RELATED

by

BLOOD

HOLLY SHEIDENBERGER

MAHONIA
— PUBLISHING —

MAHONIA
— PUBLISHING —

For the man I'll always love.

15 Years Ago

2003

1

Cleo

Some stains don't wash out.

Staring at my hands, lying face up in my lap, I know this is going to be one of them. The little girl's blood has soaked into my palms and embedded itself deep into the cracks of my fingers. The front of my yellow dress is drenched in it.

I turn to look out the rear window of his car, when Harris says, "Don't touch anything." I'm not that stupid. But I need to see the girl we're leaving behind. Floating my hands in the air as I balance my left shoulder on the seat back, I memorize the crumpled heap of a child alone on Forest Service Road 46, lying in a muck of dirt and blood. She is shrinking smaller and smaller as we drive away until the mist renders her invisible. The road is deserted, no sign of anyone coming to help her.

"Look away," Harris says. His already deep voice sounds half an octave lower than usual. I can't help but obey. "My father's people are on the way. They'll get her to a hospital. She'll be fine." His pitch is steady, but his hands grip the steering wheel so tightly he looks as though he might snap it in two. He fixes his eyes on the road ahead, intent on erasing us from the scene.

Guilt creeps up the back of my throat, but I swallow it back down. I don't want to see the incriminating reddish-brown stain on my hands as they lie there, flaccid and culpable, on my thighs.

I glance over at Harris instead. He's silent, but the air in the car is thick with the intensity of his concentration.

Just twenty minutes ago, I was gazing at him from the same angle, admiring the fine structure of his profile. But those minutes have changed us both, permanently and irrevocably.

Harris Cox has consumed my attention for the last two years. I first saw him in our sophomore psychology class at the University of Washington. I was instantly drawn to him, even from across the lecture hall. He exuded an energy, a power I couldn't describe. I wanted some of that for myself. Instead of taking lecture notes, I took mental notes of his long straight nose and smooth skin. I memorized the way his thick, dark hair swept back from his forehead in waves.

I needed to get close to him, so I made a plan.

For a full week I ditched my psych class and hid in my apartment. Then I prepared to make my entrance. Behind my ears and in my cleavage, I dabbed Black Orchid, my sultriest perfume. I put on my tightest jeans, a fitted low-cut top, and wore my long dark hair straight and glossy. I showed up early to psychology class and hovered at the back of the room until he arrived. Then I moved in and sat right behind him. As soon as there was a lull in the lecture, I leaned forward, close enough for him to smell me. Letting my hair fall over his shoulder, I whispered in his ear. "Excuse me…"

I told him I was sorry for bothering him, but I'd been out sick for a week. I just got out of the hospital, and I almost died from food poisoning. I didn't mean to intrude, but I had no other friends in the class, and I needed to borrow someone's notes. And could he please help me? The entire story was a lie, but it got me what I wanted, which was an invitation to his apartment to study.

Not much studying happened that night. There was a palpable magnetism between us. We were irresistibly attracted to each other. Kissing dissolved into foreplay, culminating in an intense, satisfying consummation. I didn't want to go home, and he didn't want me to leave, so I spent the night.

We had another "study" date later that week, and then again a few days later. Soon we didn't bother pretending to study, we just fell into a routine of spending our nights together. Four nights a week, for two years. It's the most unsettling relationship I've ever had.

I want to own him completely, but I still don't. He's my lover, but he refuses to call me his girlfriend. Is it because I don't giggle naively at his jokes, flip my hair, and hold his hand on campus? I'm not that kind of girl. I'm serious, intense, and I know what I want. I'm a thrill, and he should be grateful to have me.

Today, we were supposed to go to a secluded lake in the mountains for an out-of-character date. We usually partake of each other's company in the dark of night, not in the bright cheery light of day. But it was his idea, which makes me insatiably curious about his motive. Is he finally ready to submit to being an official couple with me?

He planned a whole day trip to Cooper Lake, which is at least a two-hour drive from Seattle, complete with a picnic lunch. He brought a gourmet basket, which he had delivered early this morning rather than packing it himself. The casual way he wears his upper-class status makes me so jealous I salivate sometimes.

I came from a humiliating background I'd rather forget. The only good thing that came from the heap of cigarette butts, empty pill bottles, and dirty fast food wrappers known as my mother is my little sister Thalia, whom I basically raised. Harris, on the other hand, is the product of a United States Senator and a pediatric surgeon from a wealthy family. While I've had to poach any social graces I could from others more fortunate than myself, he's endowed with propriety, decorum, and a trust fund.

Only about five miles of evergreen-lined road had lain between us and the lake where I was hoping he would cement our bond by bestowing on me the customary official label of "girlfriend." And then ravish me on a blanket in the open air. According to Harris, most people never travel past Cle Elum Lake, leaving Cooper Lake almost totally isolated. We expected it to be deserted today, a chilly weekday in late September.

I think he was on the cusp of the life-changing avowal when it happened.

I'd been watching Harris, admiring him silently as he drove. He turned to face me, deep brown eyes burrowing into mine. He was going to say something important. I was sure he was about to commit to me, to give himself to me completely, including the coveted label. But when he opened his mouth to speak, the sound froze in his throat. His debilitating stutter flared up, which it usually only did when he was under heavy stress. It's the one affliction this otherwise untainted human being seems to have. His lip pursed up and his eyes squeezed shut as he tried to force the word out. My own breath was bated as I anticipated what he was about to say.

I never found out because that's when we felt the thud and heard the crunch.

Harris skidded the car to a stop. He exploded a puff of air, his verbal struggle abandoned. I tore my eyes away from him, expecting to see a dead deer in the road. Blinking at the empty void in front of the car, I turned to scan the road behind me.

I heard a ghastly shriek, and I knew it had come, unauthorized, from my mouth.

Harris had run over a little girl.

Her tiny body lay contorted in the road, blood already pooling beneath her blue flowered shirt. Since I wasn't wearing a seatbelt, I was out of the car faster than Harris. I almost fell as I scrambled out the door, slipping on the wet road as I ran the forty-five yards back to her body. She was still breathing, but her eyes were closed and she wasn't responding.

Tears blurred my eyes, and I shouted to Harris to call an ambulance.

He'd gotten out and was jamming his fingers into the buttons of his BlackBerry. I scooted myself under the little girl's body and cradled her curly brown head in my hands. My voice reverted to a soothing, motherly tone I hadn't used since Thalia and I were young. "It's okay, little girl, we'll help you. You're going to be okay. Where's your mommy?" No response. I looked around, trying to discern where this little girl had come from, but all I could see was an impenetrable expanse of Douglas firs lining the road.

Harris was trying to describe our location to someone on the phone and I yelled again, trying to rush him. The child needed urgent help. Her breathing was rough and slow, and I didn't want her to die in my arms.

When Harris finished with the phone, he strode over with a serene confidence that both impressed and repulsed me. "Come on, time to go."

"What? No, we have to stay with her until the ambulance gets here." I pulled her closer, protectively.

More aggressive than I'd ever seen him, Harris grabbed my arm and tried to pull me up. "Cleo, we have to go before someone sees us with her. My father is sending someone out to take care of it."

I wasn't strong enough to resist him pulling me to my feet, but I managed to lay the girl's head down gently on the road before standing up. "What about the ambulance?"

"It'll come after we leave. But we can't be caught here." He put his hand on the small of my back and turned me away from the child. It was the first time I'd seen him in a crisis, and his placid authority aroused me. "My father will deal with this. He'll make sure the girl gets medical attention, and that we don't get into any trouble for it."

I allowed Harris to push me back to the car. I looked straight ahead, thinking I could obliterate the dreadful scene from my mind. It had been an accident. The little girl seemed to have appeared out of nowhere and wandered onto the road. It wasn't even clear where she'd come from or what she was doing all by herself.

Even so, it was Harris's fault. He'd been looking at me instead of the road.

Now, as we leave the scene, I'm re-evaluating everything I know about Harris. He seems different, suddenly. Dangerous. What else has he gotten away with? He's self-possessed, unworried that we're committing a crime by driving away from the scene of an accident. Somehow that comforts me. My reverence for him grows as I sit next to him, absorbing his confidence. That's probably evil, but it's true.

I thought I needed him before. Now I know it.

I'd always considered us equals, but now I see that Harris is much more worldly and experienced than I am. He's perfectly at ease allowing his father to rub out his mistakes with a single phone call. Senator Cox has been in office since Harris was a child, and he obviously has more power than I can fathom. My first brush with this strange world and I like it.

If I could take Harris as my husband, I could scrape off some of that power for myself. He plans to go to law school, then follow in his father's footsteps and go into politics. Gazing out at the long, forested road ahead of us, I envision a life where Harris and I are married, a power couple with an intoxicating future.

Startling me out of my trance, Harris makes an abrupt right turn. I realize I have no idea where he is taking me. "We're still going to the lake. My father's personal assistant will meet us there with some new clothes for you."

"What will we do with these?" I say, looking down at the ruined, gory dress I'm still wearing.

"She'll dispose of them."

The lake is just as deserted as we'd expected. It takes almost two hours for the Senator's assistant to arrive from Seattle. She's petite, tight-lipped, and efficient in her burgundy skirt suit. She has a bag for me. Inside is a pair of leggings, a long sleeve t-shirt, socks, underwear, and running shoes. There's even a hairbrush and an unopened package of hairbands.

When she sees my bloody hands, she retrieves a bottle of water from the car and gives it to me so I can try to rinse them off.

I strip in the tiny, smelly outhouse. When I look down, I see that the blood has stained not just my dress but my bra, my underwear, and the skin on my torso. I peel off my sticky undergarments and stuff them in the bag. I wet my hands with the few ounces of water left in the bottle. It's impossible to clean the dried blood off my body. Instead it smears, spreading over my skin even more. I use a clean corner of my destroyed yellow dress to wipe off as much as I can.

My hands refuse to dry in the cold, wet Washington air. Giving them one last wring, I put on the new clothes. They fit perfectly, even the shoes. How does Senator Cox's assistant have my sizes? After brushing my hair and pulling it up into a ponytail, I emerge from the outhouse and hand the bag to her. I'm trusting this woman to cover up the evidence of my crime. I don't even know her name.

Harris startles me by coming up behind me, spinning me around, and resting both hands on my hips. "You look downright virtuous, considering the circumstances." Only a bit of guilt darkens the pleasure Harris's approval gives me.

To quash it, I ask the prim assistant, "And the little girl? Is someone taking care of her?"

"The Senator has the situation under control. You are not to speak of this again," she says with a pointed look at me. "It's important you understand that this incident never happened."

I glance at Harris. He's unperturbed, as if he's heard this speech before.

The woman holds up the bag of my clothes soaked through with the child's blood. "These will be retained. If any information about today's events leaks out, it will be connected back to you and you alone. Mr. Cox will not be implicated. Is that clear?"

I don't understand how that could be possible, but I don't question it. I swallow the lump in my throat and nod yes. "Good," she says. She opens the trunk of the car, tosses the bag into a small metal case and locks it, then drives off without another word.

An awkward silence hangs in the damp air. What do we do now? We've just committed a hit-and-run on a child and gotten away with it. Somehow, this incident has made me want Harris more than ever. But has it damaged me in his eyes? I still don't even know what he was trying to say when he accidentally hit the girl.

Without warning, he moves close to me, so close I can feel his breath on me. He takes my face in both his hands, looks deep into my eyes and says, "Well, Cleo."

All the air rushes out of me as my tension collapses into his strong hands.

"Let's salvage what we can of this day. I'll get the picnic basket."

2

Harris

It's ruined. This fanciful pipe dream of a day.

I made a precision plan and expected to succeed. I knew I was taking a risk, but I had to. And I failed.

My father used to take me fishing at Cooper Lake as a kid. At least once a year, we'd wake up at three o'clock in the morning and drive up here before the sun rose. We'd get our boat out on the lake and fish all day, catching the biggest rainbow trout I've ever seen. Most of them we'd throw in the cooler and take home, but we'd usually gut one right there, cook it, and eat it. I've never had a better meal. Fresh fish with my father, right out of a mountain lake.

I've never wanted to share this place with anyone else. It's so secluded you feel as if you own it when you're out here alone. That's why Dad chose it. It wasn't just the majestic, snowy crags of the Cascade Mountains and the icy, placid waters framed by evergreens. He wanted a place to relax, to forget the pressures of public life for a while. I've kept this as a special place for memories with my father.

Until Cleopatra Tait came into my life.

We've been - not exactly *dating* - for about two years.

Entangled.

We've been entangled for the last two years.

She isn't good for me, and I should have broken off this relationship long ago. But I can't. I just can't stay away from her. She enthralls me. It's her aggression, the way she goes after her desires. She's like a mountain lion stalking and pouncing, then attacking and shredding until she gets every last ounce of what she wants.

Cleo's voracious quest for more out of life makes every other girl seem like a warmed-over corpse, death-walking down the inevitable path towards non-existence.

She's also ravishingly beautiful, but not in the usual uninspiring way. She has a prominent nose, and she knows how to wear it. Regal, like the queen she's named for.

She stimulates me.

She intimidates me sometimes, too, but I never show it. Exposing that type of weakness would be the quickest way to lose her. That's the one thing I cannot do.

I've debated myself on this issue endlessly since the first night she spent with me. So many times I've made a firm commitment to end this, but I've never followed through. It's not that I don't want her, it's that she's dangerous. I have an ambitious future planned. I'd be prudent to find a trophy wife. A safe woman to smile silently and blandly alongside me on the campaign trail.

I finally made an unwavering decision. Today was the day our lives would merge.

I was going to make her my wife.

My left front pants pocket is smoldering with the two-carat diamond ring I bought her. I planned to guide her to my favorite spot, with the stunning, iconic view of Chimney Rock, then pull out her hand and put the ring on her finger. No kneeling on the ground, groveling, asking permission. Not for her. Cleo needs a man who dominates her, even though we both know she's the one in control.

But now it's ruined, because of this hellish stutter of mine. The one thing I can't control.

I couldn't wait until we got here. I'd spent the entire drive drinking in Cleo's energy - her simmering, sizzling essence - and I was flooded with something I can't describe as love. It's more ferocious than love, more savage. Truer.

I turned to tell her, and everything locked up. No words, no sound, no breath. My body locked, the thought stuck in my throat, never to escape. I'm still choking on it now.

Then the sound of the little girl thudding underneath the car as I drove over her. Cleo's scream, her bloody dress, and the immortal secret that sprang up between us the second we drove away.

It's over now, the voice of reason in my head says. Cover up this crime and move on. Choose. Your woman or your future. You can always get another woman.

But not another woman like Cleo.

4 Weeks Before Election Day

2018

3

Cleo

A barrage of emotions surges through me as Harris strides onto the stage, waving and smiling at the cheering crowd. He's running for Congress.

I should be there, supporting him as his wife.

Instead, I'm home alone in my condo in the Wallingford neighborhood of Seattle, streaming the political rally live on my laptop. It's the first time he's run for political office, and I'm riveted on it. The race is tight, but I know he'll win.

More than a decade has passed since I last saw Harris in person. I still think about him incessantly. I know I should enjoy my life in the present, but I just can't seem to leave the past behind me.

That sickening accident destroyed the only chance I had at a life with him.

After the Senator's assistant left us alone at the lake that day, we stayed and had our gourmet picnic. Then Harris took me back to his high-rise apartment, where we showered together and watched all the dried blood on my body melt away and spin down the drain. We laid in his king-size bed together, mesmerized by the view of the city lights, until we fell asleep. The next morning, his phone rang before sunrise. He rolled over to answer it, then got up and took the call in the living room. When he came back, he was different.

"I have to take you home," he said.

I sat up, covering myself with the sheet. "Now?"

"Yes, now. Get dressed."

A tense, silent car ride later, I was back home in my own cheap apartment. He drove out without a word.

I sank into the too-soft cushions of my orange second-hand couch, stunned by the unexplained change in Harris. Why so brusque all of a sudden? Was it the phone call? Or did he wake up regretting the accident?

To block out the thoughts I didn't want to think, I turned on the morning news. After about two minutes, the anchor girl put on her studied alto tragedy voice to deliver a breaking story.

"A hit-and-run driver on a mountain road killed a three-year-old girl yesterday…"

Killed.

The word rang through my head.

Killed.

"…she wandered away from her family, who were hiking near the Salmon La Sac swimming hole on Forest Service Road 46…"

Killed.

Time stopped. I couldn't even hear the woman on the screen anymore. My eyes focused in like a tunnel. My stomach cramped up and my arms were shaking as I pulled them around myself.

We killed the little girl?

I was dizzy. I steadied my hands on the back of the sofa, trying not to faint.

Harris promised me his father was sending an ambulance to save her. I tried to stay with her. I held her. Her blood still stained my fingernails. I shouldn't have left her. She was dying. I didn't want to believe she was dying.

An urge came over me, and I ran to the bathroom and vomited into the toilet. Wiping my filthy mouth, I looked at myself in the mirror. My blank, loathsome face disgusted me.

I found myself with the phone in my hand, calling Harris. I tried to swallow, but my desiccated mouth just made a sick smacking sound.

His phone rang and rang, but he never picked up. I headed to class that morning, expecting him to meet me afterward as he always did, but he wasn't there. I waited all day, but he never came.

That was the end.

Harris never called me again. He never answered my messages. I'd see him across campus and try to catch his eye, but he wouldn't even wave.

He never would've abandoned me like that. I knew his father forbade him from contacting me because of the accident.

I'd lost him, and I was deep in anguish.

In the spring, about six months later, I was crossing the Quad to get to a class. He was hidden in the shade of the blossoming cherry trees, and I didn't see him until we almost crashed into each other. I've always wondered if he was waiting for me. The magnetism between us was still overpowering. Tears welling in his eyes, he looked more vulnerable than I'd ever seen him. I was desperate to grab him and kiss him until his arousal made him forget the rift between us.

Instead, he whispered, "I'm sorry," and walked out of my life forever.

I've dated other men since, but no one can captivate me the way Harris did. Harris was dangerous and commanding, enigmatic and urbane. I never got him out of my mind.

I got my master's and then doctoral degrees in psychology. Eventually, I got a position as a Psych professor at the University of Washington. Ironically, I now lecture in the same hall where Harris and I first met.

Harris completed law school as he'd planned and opened his own firm in downtown Seattle. After a few successful years, he publicly announced what I always knew was coming. He was following in his father's footsteps and running for political office.

The years haven't dulled my craving for Harris. I've read every article about him and seen every interview. He still belongs to me. Neither of us have ever married, and if it weren't for the accident, he would be mine now. He will be soon.

Every time I see the ubiquitous yard signs and endless TV commercials, I have to suppress my rage. I should be part of his life, his campaign. Instead, I'm forced to sit home alone, watching and re-watching his public appearances and press conferences on the internet just to feel close to him.

Streaming the rally on my laptop now, he takes the microphone. He still has the same wavy dark hair, with just the perfect amount of gray at the temples. I lean in to get a closer look at the screen.

Something is wrong. He's smiling, but I can tell it's not genuine. His eyes are troubled, and he looks uptight. He takes three slow, deep breaths, causing a long, uncomfortable silence. But the moment passes, and he clears his throat and launches into his speech.

I lie down on the tan leather couch and close my eyes, letting his deep voice wash over me. Everybody else hears his five-point plan for restoring responsibility in Washington, but I hear him declaring his passion and begging forgiveness for abandoning me all these years.

Mid-sentence, Harris goes silent.

The break in speech rhythm shocks me out of my fantasy. I peer at him on my laptop screen. Disaster has struck.

Harris's stutter is back, and he's having a full-blown speech block on stage at the rally. I know this was always his biggest fear, but I've followed every moment of his career and it's never happened in public. Since I wasn't paying attention to his words, I don't know what he's trying to get out, but he's definitely stuck. His lips are pursed like he's trying to make a sound, and he's pushing to get it out. His eyes are bugging, and he's not breathing. I hold my breath as I am sucked into the scene, silently rooting for him.

His eyes look terrified, and he blinks wildly a few times. I gasp and my hand flies to my mouth as I watch him sway, then slump to the floor with a soft thud. Acting on pure instinct, I leap to my feet as if that will give me a better view of him. People are swarming the stage, and his campaign manager takes the microphone to get control of the crowd. The internet feed cuts out abruptly, leaving me gaping at a blank screen.

I have to see Harris.

Throwing on a jacket, I grab my handbag and keys, not knowing where I am going. Once in my car, I reason that he'll be taken to a hospital. The most advanced facility nearby is the University hospital, so I drive over there as quickly as possible without being stopped for speeding.

The hospital is bustling as usual, but there's no sign of any extra security or VIP patients. I know I won't get any information from the check-in desk, but one of my professor colleagues has connections with the medical personnel here. I text her, asking how I can find Harris. A few minutes pass, until she pulls some strings and gets me connected with Harris's staff.

I take the elevator up to the appropriate floor and meet Harris's Head of Security, who's posted outside the door to his room. He's large and intimidating, but I march up to him and tell him I'm an old friend and I'm sure Harris will want to see me. I pace back and forth while the guard is inside the room. I'm sweating, but I'm ice cold. The possibility that Harris will refuse to see me is unbearable.

The guard comes back out. "You can have fifteen minutes." He jerks his thumb towards the open door.

A sob of joy almost escapes, but I choke it back. I smooth my hair, unbutton an extra button at the top of my shirt, and glide into the room.

There he is. He's sitting up in bed, looking not just healthy but downright virile. My breath catches in my throat. All the need I've buried comes rushing to the surface, threatening to consume me. It takes all my self-restraint to keep from jumping onto his bed and making love to him right there. Instead, I exhale and pull a chair up to the bed, sitting as close as I can.

"Are you all right?" After fantasizing about this moment for fifteen years, it's the only thing I can think to say. Pathetically unimaginative. "I saw you at the rally..." I add lamely.

"You came," he says, silencing me. His commanding presence transcends the hospital bed he's reclining in.

"I had to," I say. "You're everywhere. The ads, the

posters. I missed you so much after…"

"Don't." He scoots to the edge of the bed, where he can reach me. He rests his hand on my knee, sending an electric thrill through me. "I missed you, too."

He doesn't remove his hand, but lets it linger on my thigh. A long pause passes between us as I breathe deeply, savoring his touch. So much is unspoken, but it's too dangerous to speak aloud.

"Is it okay for me to be here with you now?" I hate the timidness in my voice. I'm praying he won't dismiss me. Now more than ever, he still can't risk anyone finding out that we killed that little girl.

"Why do you think I pulled that stunt at the rally today?" He grins roguishly. "It's not easy to get your attention."

He's playing this off like the politician he is, but I need the truth. Overcome with anxiety, I ask, "What happened to you?" His fainting today showed uncharacteristic weakness. "Are you sick?"

Harris looks down at the blanket on his lap, and his voice gets quiet. "No." He picks at the lint. "I'm not sick." He sighs, then shifts back to his jocular banter. "Pretty embarrassed, though. Can't be passing out on the campaign trail like a freshman at his first college party, now can I?"

"You'll have to hold another press conference to explain yourself, Mr. Future Congressman."

His mood darkens again. "Yes, I suppose that's true. Maybe I'll have my campaign manager do it."

I boldly reach out and put my palm on his chest, relishing the still-familiar feel of his body. I don't know how, but I will find out what's going on with Harris. He closes his eyes and exhales. He doesn't touch me back, but he doesn't push me away.

4

Harris

I gave her my personal cell phone number. I shouldn't have.

She only stayed the fifteen minutes I allotted, but I couldn't resist her even for that long. The moment she breezed into this oppressive, sterile room, I exhaled more fully than I have in years. The stubborn tension in my shoulders and neck evaporated. The dull, ever-present ache behind my left eye floated away. My body missed her more than my mind even realized.

But I never could have gotten this far if I hadn't left her.

What chaos have I summoned into my carefully structured life by permitting her to contact me? I can't afford any disruption in the next four weeks. The polls are uncomfortably close, and bouncing back from yesterday's humiliating disaster will be challenging enough.

I can't, shouldn't, *won't*, talk to her.

Out of a sense of duty to myself and responsibility to the army of people counting on me to get elected, I vow not to have any further contact with Cleo, no matter how relentless she may be.

My decision is firm.

I mean what I say.

But I don't trust myself.

My own will betrays me. I *want* to see her again.

I pick up my phone and scroll through the contacts. Her name jumps out at me as if it's printed in bold. How can I stop myself from contacting her when she's only a tap away?

I must not, and yet I must.

I am a pitiful, weak-willed fool.

5

Cleo

I talked Harris into having dinner with me, Thalia, and her husband Warren tonight. I'd rather have him all to myself, but he was reluctant to come to my place. Next time he will.

I'm waiting for him outside my sister's house because he didn't want to ride with me. I don't blame him. The last time we were together in a car was the day after the accident that tore our lives in half.

I'm about to recapture Harris, and when I do, I will not let him get away again. I will never go back to the tedious, insipid existence I led during the fifteen years without him.

Sunday morning after his collapse, he was released with a clean bill of health. Freshly showered and shaved, he flashed his brilliant smile at the camera crews waiting outside the hospital. I watched him on the local morning news. His explanation that he had collapsed from exhaustion, but was well-rested now and "ready to get back to working hard for the American people" seems to have satisfied everyone. Except me.

He still hasn't told me the truth. It isn't normal to lose consciousness and slump into a heap on the floor in the middle of a public appearance. I'm suppressing the urge to worry that he has some undisclosed fatal disease, because I can't tolerate the thought that I might lose him again.

He arrives in his silver Audi, gets out, and treats me to that dazzling politician's smile. My breath catches as I take in that handsome, slightly lined face. I ask, "You ready for this? My sister's kids can be a little... challenging."

Seeing my two nieces is always a strain on me. I had intended to raise children of my own someday, but the accident changed that. Now every time I see a little girl I flash back to holding that tiny curly head in my lap as the blood flowed out, taking the life with it.

Harris isn't concerned. "Up for the challenge," he says, flashing his grin again. "I love kids."

"Let's do it, then." He places his hand on my lower back and the electricity between us is so powerful I catch my breath. He drops his hand as quickly as if it had been burned. Our eyes sink into each other, crumbling the walls of time. I want him, and I know he wants me, too.

Later.

Side by side, we head up the walk to my sister's front door.

Thalia and Warren live in a cramped, depression-era house in Ballard. It's the only one left on the block. All the other lots host million-dollar mini mansions built in the last five years. Once inside, my nieces attack Harris with their usual adrenalized exuberance. They jump up and down, shrieking at each other's silly jokes. Harris endures their clinging leg hugs with all the charm of a winning politician.

Thalia is in her element hosting the dinner. She strives to make Harris feel comfortable, and he seems genuinely charmed by this raucous, homey environment. No doubt it's foreign to his experience, growing up the only child in a strict, but privileged household.

Harris is the perfect dinner guest. He's charismatic, witty, and smart. He entertains the table with self-deprecating stories, laughs at Warren's dull attempt at humor, jabbers with the girls about their favorite cartoons, and thanks my sister graciously for her hospitality.

As soon as dinner is over and the girls are put to bed, Thalia wastes no time serving coffee. It's awful. Over-roasted, over-extracted, and dark as charcoal. Embarrassing for a native Seattleite, but whatever disdain Harris might have doesn't show.

As I sip it, I feel my lip curl. My eyes squint and my jaw clenches as I peer across the room at my sister chattering at Harris. The evening has been pleasant enough, but I've had no chance to talk to him alone since we got here. Was this a mistake? I should have insisted he meet me alone.

Not one to squander an opportunity, Warren cuts in on Thalia and Harris's conversation. He sequesters Harris in the corner, most likely airing his complaints about the government. Warren runs his own restaurant, and I don't think it's doing very well. He's the kind of person who blames everyone and everything other than himself when things aren't working.

Eavesdropping on their conversation, I hear "taxes" and "minimum wage" and other key phrases volleyed back and forth. I'm sure Warren is lodging his grievances about business and tax law, expecting Harris to promise him favors once he's elected. Despite being hopelessly uneducated, Warren has a gift for trapping someone in a conversation. Harris will be captive for a while, so I take the opportunity to catch up with my sister.

Thalia elbows me in the rib. "Harris looks gorgeous," she says. "How long has it been since he broke your heart?"

She knows nothing about the accident and the dead girl. Not one word about it ever escaped my lips to anyone. I let her think Harris dumped me for some unknown and therefore unjust reason. Since she unfailingly takes my side in everything, she's always referred to him as "that cold-blooded snake." Tonight's the first time I've heard her call him by his name.

"Fifteen years," I answer. "But that's in the past. Now... he's even more intriguing than he was before. Older, smarter, more in control."

"And even more charming, if that's possible," says Thalia. "He's certainly got Warren wrapped around his little finger."

We share a laugh and I ask her how things are going with her and Warren. She recoils with a grimace as if I'd just thrown a pie in her face. "Not good. Finances, mostly," she says.

"How not good?"

"Like, the restaurant has been nothing but a sinkhole of debt. It was working for the first year or so, when it was new. But that first push wore off and Warren just hasn't been able to turn it around."

"But at least it's breaking even?" I ask.

"I wish," says Thalia.

"What are you going to do? Can you keep it open?"

She leans in and says in a hoarse whisper, "I don't even care about that God-forsaken place right now. What I care about is keeping my house."

"Oh my God, Thal. Are you in that much trouble?"

"Yes," she says. "I've talked to Warren about it, but he doesn't want to hear it. Honestly, he is so frustrating. Impossible, actually. I've started to hate him. Really, truly hate him. He makes me so crazy I've even wished Mom was alive so I could take the girls and go live with her."

"That *is* crazy."

I had no idea she was in danger of losing her house. She and Warren have always projected the image of being the perfect couple. But I know better than anyone how unexpectedly a relationship can be torn apart.

"I'm thinking about going back to work," she says.

"What would you do? Go back to office work?"

"That would make the most sense, but I can't. What would I do with the girls? There's no one to take care of them when they're not in school... Winter Vacation, Spring Break, the whole summer. Full-time childcare is so expensive, it's completely out of the question."

"Can you find a babysitter, just for the hours that you need them, so you can go back to work?"

Thalia sighs. "The problem is... I don't want to. I want to leave Warren."

I didn't think my good girl little sister could shock me, but she just did. I actually thought she and Warren were happy. She certainly has hidden it well. Judging by her social media accounts, life is just one sunny, filtered moment after another.

"I want to help you, Thal. You know I'll always be here for you. What do you need most right now?"

"Money," she says. "I need our mortgage paid. It's three months behind, and if it isn't paid by the end of this month, we're going into foreclosure."

"Done." I have plenty of money in savings. I stash

money away like a pack rat, always have, even though I'm practically guaranteed a job since I'm tenured. My sister is the only family I have left in the world, and I raised her. I'd do anything for her.

Plus, I can't have her asking if she and the girls can move in with me.

"Will ten thousand take care of it?"

Thalia's face is white. She obviously didn't expect me to fix her problem so quickly. "Ten grand is more than enough. It's too much, actually. I can't let you do that. This is Warren's mess."

"I want to help you. It's not for Warren, it's for you and the girls, so you can stay in your house. Give me your account number before I leave today, and I'll transfer it by tomorrow morning. Then you can take care of whatever you need to take care of. And you let me know if you need anything else. I'm here for you, Sis."

Just as she's giving me a grateful hug, Harris saunters over. He must have had his fill of Warren's ramblings on politics and what's wrong with business today. He looks relaxed, though. I've noticed when he's on the campaign trail he always wears that toothpaste-commercial smile and an overdone confidence. It's an act I never remember him pulling with me when we were alone together.

Now, though, after an evening with me, my sister, and her family, his bearing is effortless and natural. He looks almost vulnerable, but I know he's still the same commanding, invincible man he appears to be on television. Power and sensitivity are a deadly combination in a man. My attraction to him escalates out of control. I need this man. We have to put this accident behind us because I can't live without him any longer.

"I'm afraid I have to head home now. I've got an appearance early tomorrow morning. Cleo?"

"Of course," I answer.

"Thank you both for a wonderful evening." He directs his comment to Thalia, ignoring Warren. He rests his hand on her shoulder. "I sincerely hope we can do it again sometime." My sister blushes.

"That would be lovely," she says.

While everyone exchanges handshakes and hugs, she presses a small piece of paper into my palm and whispers, "I owe you." I look to confirm that it's her account number before pocketing it without anyone seeing.

Harris and I leave the house together, pausing in the driveway before parting ways. He thanks me for "a lovely evening." He looks deeply into my eyes, and I know he feels the same way I do. I drive home giddy, even though we never got any quality time alone tonight.

Soon.

6

Harris

The influence my father wields over me cannot be overstated. He's been a U.S. Senator for most of my life, so he's always been a busy, important man. Because he was frequently away, I treasured any time I could get with him. The first thing he always did when he got home from his condo in Virginia was take me for a walk down the tree-lined path near our house. Side by side, I could talk to him about anything. Had we sat face to face over dinner at a crowded restaurant, I would have been far too self-conscious to talk about my most private issues. But on these walks, I've shared my deepest feelings with my father, the man I admire most.

I've always wanted to be like him. Having come from a poor family, he brought himself up by his bootstraps. He established a successful career as an attorney, which meant that I grew up in privilege. Because I've never known the same hardships, I have none of the life experience that resonates so strongly with his constituents. He exhibits a level of compassion I've never found inside myself. I've learned to fake it for the cameras, but never authentically feel it.

We're taking one of our walks today. He made an unscheduled trip home to spend time with me. Of course, my damned collapse made national news. My father knew before I even called him from the hospital. Later that night, we talked on the phone and he gave me some advice on drafting up my statement for the press conference I had to give the next day. I don't know whether the damage to my image has been fixed, but having my father here is encouraging.

We walk in silence for a while, letting the atmosphere between us settle. We always do this after not talking for a while. He usually lets me go first, wisely, to let me direct where I want the conversation to go. Today I don't know how to say all the things I want to say. I want to be strong and powerful and stable like my father. But inside I'm carrying so much fear. I'm like a terrified child. That's why I collapsed. Fear. Cowardice. Not exhaustion, like I said in my public statement. My father knows that, but he wants me to admit it, both to him and to myself.

I take a deep breath and dive in. "Dad, do you know why I fainted?"

My father answers me in his deep, self-assured voice. "I believe I do, Son. But I also believe you need to tell me yourself."

Focusing on my breathing as he trained me to do years ago, I say, "I was afraid, Dad."

"Afraid of...?" He leaves the question hanging, expecting the answer he already knows.

"I have this increasing dread that everyone is going to find out about my stutter. I've been having dreams where I get completely blocked and can't physically speak at all. I wake up in a cold sweat and can't get back to sleep."

"And then it happened," he said. "Your worst nightmare came true."

"Yes. I'd practiced my speech in advance, but I kept thinking about those nightmares. My anxiety got out of control. I was tense, and clenching, and holding my breath. I was literally paralyzed with panic. All I could see were the bright lights, and then I got dizzy and fell down. I completely lost consciousness."

"In front of everyone, on television."

"Yes," I puff.

"Harris, we have discussed this before." He's stoic as always. A rock. "You can do this. We worked through your stutter together when you were a young man. You're an adult now. A professional, an attorney, a businessman, and soon to be a congressman. You achieved all this while working with and through your speech disfluencies. When was the last time you had a serious block?"

I think back, and I can't remember the last time I had a truly debilitating block, other than at the rally. It must have been before law school. I told him so.

"Well then, it's time you accept the confidence you deserve. You are a man who used to stutter, not a man who stutters."

"Except for the rally—"

"Yes, Son, except for the rally. It was an exception, not a new normal." He claps me on the back and grins at me. "Now, what else can we talk about? Not work, what about privately? It's tough to keep your private life happy when you're campaigning. I know that better than anybody. How are you doing?"

Should I tell him about the woman who has just come in to my life? Or, more accurately, *back* into my life? I could keep this to myself, but I appreciate my father's advice and good counsel. Besides, he's always harassing me about finding a beautiful wife to hang on my arm, to take to those inevitable Washington parties.

"Well, there's this woman..." I start out. He bursts out in a gale of hearty laughter.

"It's always a woman, isn't it, Son? Tell me about her. She'd better be a special one."

I'm conscious of the fact that I can't tell him who it is, because he will not approve of me associating with her publicly. He'll tell me all about the dangers of being with her, how it'll harm my reputation and probably even lose me the campaign. He'd be right, of course. I know it's all wrong, but I haven't felt this way in years. I'm captivated in a way I can't remember being, at least not for a very long time.

"She's enchanting, Dad. A truly special woman. I'm intrigued, and I can't stop thinking about her."

"Do I know her?"

"I'd rather keep it under wraps for now, because nothing is official. But I will say that my collapse was what brought us together. I spent some time with her last week. It was the most at ease I've felt in a long time. I would like to have spent some more time alone with her, but it just wasn't possible at the time."

"Sounds great. I can't wait to hear more about her. Once you've made things official, of course. Now, the election is only a couple of weeks away. Have you only seen her in a private setting so far?"

I'm nervous about Dad's questions. I'm not accustomed to keeping things from him, but I'm certain that he won't approve of me getting anywhere near her. So to appease him I say, "Yes. Definitely only in private."

"If I can offer a bit of counsel, from experience?" he asks.

I nod. "Please."

"Keep a lid on this thing until after you win the

election. I'm sure she's a wonderful woman, and I know how hard it is to keep your mind off a woman once you've started falling for her. Believe it or not, I still remember those days with your mother. But you can't afford any disruption to your image in this final stretch. No contact until after you win. Period."

My father's right, of course. With my fainting like a scared little girl at the rally last week, my poll numbers have slipped and I can't afford any setbacks. In order to win, I have to rebound hard and fast. I've got to get my numbers back up to where they were before. It was a tight race before, but I'm dangerously close to being on the wrong side of the split now. Regardless, he is right.

"Thanks, Dad. I'll keep things under control. Nothing public until after the win."

3 Weeks Before Election Day

7

Cleo

I'm suffering from the very affliction I should be writing about. My laptop is open, waiting for me to type some brilliant paragraphs on the subject of infatuation for a seminar I'll be giving at the University. Unfortunately, my focus is seriously impaired by the object of my own affections, one Harris Cox.

Last week's dinner keeps replaying over and over in my mind, intensifying my desire for him. The strong, solid feel of him next to me at the table, the surprising seductiveness of his eyes crinkling when he laughed. He wears maturity well.

The desperate fear that keeps surfacing, no matter how often I rebury it, is that he is repulsed by me. He hasn't taken me to bed. He hasn't asked me to spend the night, or even tried to kiss me. I tell myself it's because he's a gentleman, but I know that's a lie. Harris Cox gets what he wants, and he doesn't want me.

He's not the first. In the lonely silence of my condo, the ghosts of past relationships haunt me. There was Andrew, who split up with me in front of his employees just because I visited him at his office without texting first. Yes, it was the third time in a week, but he had no right to humiliate me like that. He was boring, anyway.

Mateo was sexier and more spontaneous. The three weeks we spent together were a non-stop romp, but he walked out on me in the middle of the night when he said I slapped him too hard. I challenged him to slap me back harder, but he just yanked his pants on and left.

Ryan is the only guy who wants me. Maybe a little too much. But it's time for Ryan to go. I'll push him out of the way to make room for Harris.

If Harris rejects me...

No. We're meant to be together. Our destinies intertwine and I won't let them unravel. If it hadn't been for that wretched accident, we would've been married by now. I can't expect him to initiate a physical relationship when he's campaigning for a major public office. The election is in just a few weeks and as soon as he wins, he'll be mine. I know he wants that as much as I do.

Maybe he'll even propose to me the night of the election. At the victory party. That would be stunning, if he did it in front of so many people. Maybe even on camera. I'll squeeze out tears and everyone will love me.

Like a wrecking ball, it hits me. I have nothing to wear.

I have to start thinking seriously about being a congressman's wife. Flinging my closet doors open, I realize my wardrobe is pathetically bland. The row of neutral slacks and solid color button-up shirts screams professor. Functional, professional, and dull. It appears that I've lost my edge in the fashion department.

What should I wear as the wife of a congressman? Tailored pantsuits? Skirt and blouse with jacket? Harris's wife needs to be enviably gorgeous, not academic.

I spend a good hour pawing through the dark corners of my tiny closet, even opening the sweater bins on the top shelf. Finally, I put together three ensembles that I look smashing in. They all fit into a strict color palette: blood red, black, and gray. Sophisticated, smart, yet sexy with a hint of danger. I slide on the deep red dress that I bought for a New Year's Eve party a few years ago, pull my dark hair back, and admire myself in the mirror. Though my usual look doesn't show it, my workout routine has definitely paid off. My body looks fabulous, if I do say so myself. I was right to stick with it, even when it didn't matter before. It certainly does now.

I push the deep red fitted dress shirt with gray skirt and jacket to the front of the closet, along with the black crew-neck fitted cashmere sweater and black pencil skirt and my highest black heels. I am ready for Mr. Harris Cox, future congressman and future husband.

Still wearing the hot red dress, I remember the last photo I took with Harris. We took a self-portrait with an old-fashioned film camera on the day we went to the lake, after the accident. He's holding me, smiling, with the majestic Chimney Rock perfectly framed in the background. I didn't get it developed until months later, but there's no mistaking it. The date is even printed right on the photo. It's always brought back a disturbing muddle of emotions. The last blissful moment before he left me forever.

At first I'd looked at that picture every day, praying that Harris would crawl back to me like a dying man in the desert begging for water. He never came. One night I hid it at the bottom of my underwear drawer before another man came over, and it's been there ever since. I never could give it up, though. Because I never could give up Harris.

Knowing exactly where the picture is, I rummage around the bottom of the drawer until I come up with it. It's old, faded, and bent at the corners, but still exactly as I remember it. A perfect frozen moment with my lover, just before he's ripped away from me. We look shockingly untroubled, considering that we had just killed a child. I was lying to myself, pretending she was going to be all right.

In the unexplored darkness of my soul, I know the truth. I cared about keeping Harris far more than I ever cared about saving that little girl. If she had to die for me to be with him, then so be it. Is that evil? Or is it love?

I stick the photo to my bathroom mirror. Right in the center at eye level. I can't see my own reflection anymore, just him.

Having taken the edge off my anxiety about Harris, I grab my phone and call my sister. "Hi, Thal," I say. "I wanted to check in on you. Did the funds transfer come through okay?"

"Yes, Cleo. I can't thank you enough for helping us out." She sighs laboriously. "I'll pay you back as soon as I get the chance, but I don't know how Warren is going to pull this off. The whole thing is so—"

"Don't fret. I can afford it, and I want you and the girls to be safe, whatever you decide to do about Warren." Even though I hate putting myself in such a vulnerable position, I pose the question I fear the answer to. "Can I ask you something about dinner with Harris last week?"

Thalia hesitates before answering. "Sure. I guess."

"Did you... get a sense that Harris is... interested in me?"

The question hangs in the air long enough to make me uncomfortable. She finally says, "That's kind of a surprising question. I thought you two had a thing back in college and he dumped you."

"It wasn't exactly like that." My voice has an unintended, hostile edge to it. I try to soften it, saying, "It would be fun to get together again, wouldn't it? I mean, if you'd like to."

Thalia brightens like the sun coming over the horizon. "Yes, that's a spectacular idea. I would really love to hang out with you and Harris again. The three of us. No Warren."

"Okay, no Warren."

She lets out a giggle that makes me realize where my nieces get it from. She's genuinely excited about the three of us getting together again.

Somehow, I'm not.

Despite what I just offered, that's not going to happen.

Next time I see Harris, we're going to be alone.

8

Harris

Driving home, I'm about a block away in my car when I see her. A woman sitting on my front porch step.

I bought this house on lower Queen Anne Hill when I chose the Congressional district I wanted to represent. It was designed in Frank Lloyd Wright's prairie style, streamlined, angular, with a dramatic horizontal roof. It's perfect for me. Pale gray trimmed in burgundy, with a view overlooking the Seattle city lights. I've never had a guest in it.

I'm still too far away to recognize the woman from here. Could it be...? I pull a little closer in my car and slow down. My security team's not with me now, so I can't be too careful. It's Cleo. Of course.

I stop in front of the porch and roll down the window. "Cleo? Why are you here?"

She stands and holds up a white paper bag. "I brought you dinner. I thought you could use some company."

Knowing Cleo does nothing without a motive, I'm morbidly curious about her true intentions. And she has something I want. "Let me park and I'll come around," I say.

Heading to my front porch from the garage in back, I'm apprehensive. My heart is racing and I have to admit this woman unnerves me. I'm afraid of falling under her spell and losing all control. The thought occurs to me that I never told her where I live. How did she find my house? Seductive and resourceful. Dangerous combination.

She looks like she wants to undress me right here on the porch, but she restrains herself.

"Thai food, your favorite," she says. "At least it used to be."

"Still is," I say. "Come on in the house."

I sit down at the small, sleek table in my slate-colored kitchen. I'm not accustomed to having a woman in my house. It's been a long time since I had a relationship serious enough to bring someone home.

Cleo makes herself right at home, bustling about my kitchen, finding plates in the cabinets and putting out the disposable chopsticks. She dumps the food out of the cartons onto the plates. I don't bother helping because I'm amused by her attempt at domesticity. She's got a plate in each hand and she spins around like a sassy diner waitress. I have to admit, she looks great. She's kept her figure. In fact, she's fitter than she was in college. She obviously works out.

"Pad Thai, two stars," she says, smiling. "Not too spicy for you. Weak."

"Actually, I take three stars now," I say. "Maybe even four." It's not true; spicy food feels like a punishment to me. But being called weak is even worse.

It's both unsettling and satisfying to see Cleo again. It's like we're a two-piece jigsaw puzzle and we fit together to complete a darkly odd picture. For the last fifteen years,

I've been running away from my missing piece and now it's found me.

I never wanted to desert her after the accident. It was my father's idea, and of course he was right. It was too risky to be seen with her anymore, knowing what had happened the day of the accident. The poor family never found out who hit their little girl, but Cleo and I got away with it. If my father hadn't forced me to separate from her, I never would've found the courage to leave her. And I wouldn't be on the verge of becoming a congressman now. Life has been much less treacherous without her.

The risk isn't entirely gone, but I can't deny how natural it feels to be alone with her. Like it was pre-destined by some unseen force.

"So, tell me everything," I say, before digging into my food. "About your life. What have I missed over the last fifteen years?" I was so focused on putting her behind me, I haven't kept up with her at all. She found out where I live, but I didn't even know she was still in Washington. She hasn't moved away, but I don't know what career she ended up in.

"I assume you're not currently married, since you don't wear a ring," I say. Immediately, I kick myself for making such a politically incorrect comment. I never would've done that on the campaign trail. This woman's got me off guard. I backpedal as quickly as I can. "Not that you need to wear a ring to symbolize your belonging to a man..."

She smirks. She knows she's caught me in a self-laid trap.

"No, Harris, I'm not married." She leans across the table toward me, her red blouse undone just one button too far. "I've never been married, and neither have you. Don't you find that peculiar?"

I can't possibly argue with her. "Of course, it's

peculiar," I play along. "We're two very attractive adults. I know I'm wildly successful, but I notice you haven't admitted to your line of work yet. Embarrassing, is it?"

"No, not at all. I happen to be a valuable member of society, not some sleazy politician lawyer scum like you."

"Well, don't keep me waiting. Out with it."

"I'm a psychology professor at the University of Washington. It just so happens that I lecture in the same hall where I first lured you into inviting me to your apartment."

I didn't expect her to bring up our past. My stomach lurches as I'm instantly transported back to college. She was just as fascinating then as she is now. So dangerous and unusual. I had never met another girl like her.

The day she came up behind me and whispered seductively in my ear... everything about it is still so clear. I wanted her right away. I couldn't leave her alone, even though I knew she was all wrong for me. She was never going to be a good political wife. Not well-behaved enough.

I'm glad my father insisted we part after the accident. If he hadn't, I may never have freed myself from her. She was too magnetic and my desire was too strong.

But now here she is, invading my space. Again. What am I going to do with this woman?

I doubt my ability to extricate myself from her of my own free will. I certainly can't ask my father to help me like he did back then. She's hooked me like a fish, and she's about to reel me in.

"I was in love with you, you know," she says.

Her bluntness startles me. Shouldn't, I suppose. She's always been like that. She's challenging me, testing to see how I'll respond.

"You didn't know what love was," I say.

"True," she counters. "Wanted you, then."

"What exactly did you want?"

"To own you." Her eyes bore into mine. This woman means business. "I still want that."

"As a politician, I have to tell you officially that I'm not for sale," I say.

"I wasn't offering to pay," she says, getting up from the table. "You'll excuse me while I borrow your restroom. Don't miss me while I'm gone."

"I won't," I promise.

As soon as she latches the door, I get up as quietly as I can and steal over to the living room, where she left her phone lying on the coffee table. I'm surprised, but pleased to find it isn't locked. I scroll through until I find what I'm looking for, then snap a photo of her screen with my phone. Before she opens the bathroom door, I'm back in my seat at the table.

"Now you're going to tell me what happened to you at the rally last week," she says as soon as she's sitting across from me again. It's a command rather than a question. Has this woman always been so forward? "The truth," she says.

Something about her relentless pursuit of what she wants bewitches me. She disarms me and makes me feel comfortable, even though I know she's the furthest thing from safe. She's going to be the death of me, but I can't help myself.

I take a deep breath. "You want to know the darkest secrets of Harris Cox?"

"Yes." She doesn't blink.

"You already know about my stutter. That is my darkest secret."

"No, it isn't. That's not why you fainted."

"Collapsed," I correct her. "And yes, it is the reason. Indirectly. The doctors have diagnosed me with something called 'glossophobia.' That's basically a fancy name for a crippling fear of public speaking. Ironic for a politician."

"And lawyer," she says.

"Yes, and that." I shift in my chair. This topic gives me severe anxiety, but I continue on. "I'm terrified of people finding out. About the stutter. It's become paralyzing for me. I almost can't function anymore when I have to speak in public. And then at the rally..."

I look up at her and I can feel my eyes wide and wet. I'm fighting the urge to break down, but I'm so vulnerable with her. She owns me, even if she doesn't know it yet. "I couldn't do it, Cleo. I couldn't speak at all. I panicked. Nothing would come out, no matter what I did. I pushed and pushed, not breathing, until finally I just... fainted." I finish in a whisper.

"Collapsed," she whispers back. She reaches across the table to cover my hand with hers. It's warm and comforting. How can one woman be so right and yet so wrong?

9

Cleo

Ryan is scheduled to be in my office in five minutes, which means he'll be here in three. He's eager, that one. We've been dating for only a couple of months, but he's gotten very attached. I found out after the fact that he's never slept with anyone besides me. If I'd known, I never would've pursued him.

The fact that he's my student has complicated things. I've stayed with him longer than I would have because I can't risk angering him. He could ruin my career. It's in my contract not to consort with students. The fact remains, though, that a very real sexual attraction exists between us.

There's his knock.

"Ryan, come in," I say, completely professional until the door is closed behind him. He smells good, freshly showered and shaved. I breathe in his scent and reconsider the purpose of this meeting.

I grab his wrists and walk backwards, pulling him with me, until I'm sitting on top of my desk straddling him with my thighs. With no serious contemplation, I've already decided to put off my declaration until after we have a little fun. I lean back over my desk, which I keep meticulously neat, and pull Ryan down on top of me. Kissing him, smelling him, running my hands through his still-damp hair, I don't regret my decision to have one last libidinous fling before I dump him.

Forty-five minutes later, we are lying on the floor, both rumpled and breathless. Ryan is good. I've trained him well. I dare say he's blossoming from an awkward psych student into what could almost be called a proper young stallion. I don't think I'd let Ryan go if I wasn't mad for Harris Cox.

But I am.

Catching my breath, I turn my head and look into Ryan's deep brown eyes. "You've gotten very good at this, Ryan. I'd say that rose almost to the level of high art."

"I'm privileged to have such a great teacher," he says. "I'm still eager to learn as much as I can from you."

I rise to a sitting position, then struggle to stand up while smoothing my tight skirt back into place. "There won't be any more lessons, Ryan." I unzip my skirt to tuck in my blouse. "Consider that an early graduation present. You're an expert now, and you don't need me anymore."

He looks up at me from the floor like a beaten dog. "Are you… breaking up with me?"

"In a manner of speaking," I say.

Jumping to face me, looking childish with his hair all mussed, Ryan's eyes are wild. "But I—" He swallows and blinks hard a few times. "I think I love you, Cleo."

This is unexpected. I knew he'd gotten quite attached, and was exclusive with me even though we had made no actual commitment to each other, but he certainly had never declared love. I glance at the clock. We've been in my office for nearly an hour now, and I have about six minutes to get him out of here. We only meet here, and always keep our silent trysts under an hour so that I could claim it was nothing more than a closed-door student consultation during office hours.

"No, you don't, Ryan. You're confusing sexual attraction with love. You're transferring your feelings onto me simply because you've never been with another woman sexually. As soon as—"

He grabs my arm, hard. "Don't you start psycho-analyzing me. I know you, inside and out, and I want you." I squirm to get out of his grasp, but he's too strong. This aggressive side of Ryan is new, and it frightens me. I need him out of here without causing a scene. Since he physically overpowers me, my best bet is to play along.

I let my body soften and fall into an S-curve. "What do you want to do with me...?" I ask, tilting my head and licking the corner of my upper lip.

He kisses me possessively. I kiss him back, eyes open, looking at the clock on the wall behind him.

"That, for starters," he says. "What do you think about that?"

"I think I've created a monster." Pulling away, I slap him hard across the face. "I told you, this is over. Leave now, or I cry rape."

He's shaking with what I guess is a combination of disbelief and rage. He reaches behind him for the doorknob, turns it without breaking my gaze, and then whirls around and stalks out.

10

Harris

"Harris! You look darling!"

Before I can even react, she's got her arms around my neck and she's squeezing me tighter than her tiny frame would indicate she could. She smells like honeysuckle. Sweet, charming, and fresh. Just like her.

Amber Lindstrom.

She's about ten years younger than me, and it's been longer than that since I last saw her. Our fathers go way back. Over the years, we'd see each other at social functions, and she'd always tag along behind me like an eager puppy. Eventually, I figured out that she had an incurable crush on me, so I kept my distance. She was cute, but I never saw her as anything other than a smitten kid.

My father was the one who put today's visit on my campaign schedule. He arranged all the details of when and where I was to go, but he neglected to prepare me for grown-up Amber. She is… incredibly appealing. Shiny blonde hair and clear blue eyes in a perfect petite package.

A classic beauty from an influential family. The ideal candidate for a proper politician's wife. My father knows what he's doing.

I find my eyes roving over her body, imagining how she looks underneath her impeccably tailored skirt and blouse. Tempting.

Amber pulls back and smiles. Her teeth are perfect, too. Of course.

"Lovely to see you again, Amber. It's been too long."

"Harris, you silly goose, don't be so formal. It's me!"

She punches me lightly in the arm, and for some reason, I love it.

"Well, put me to work," I say, trying - and failing - to match her energy level.

Having wealthy parents affords many privileges, one of which is never having to get a job. Amber runs a charity that provides health care to underprivileged women and their children. They're hosting a free check-up day at the neighborhood elementary school today, and my father offered me up as a volunteer. Of course, a news crew will be covering it. Can't let a good publicity opportunity go to waste.

I roll up my sleeves, unbutton my shirt collar, and prepare to get to work.

For the cameras, anyway.

Amber grabs my hand and drags me to a storage room adjacent to the auditorium. She unlocks it, flips on the light, and says, "Voila! Your duty awaits, Sir."

The room is full of folding chairs. So many folding chairs. Hundreds. Tables, too. Amber explains that I have an hour to set them all up in the auditorium. She says, "Get going, big fella." Then smiles, winks, and prances away.

Something about Amber's enthusiasm destroys my willpower to protest.

An hour later, the tables are arranged. The chairs are set. And I'm sweating like I just ran the Seattle Marathon. To make matters worse, the news crew just arrived.

Fortunately, I carry an extra pressed shirt in my car for just such occasions. I retrieve it, take it to the bathroom, and change. Roll the sleeves up again, for effect. Got to look like I've been working. My damp hair adds to the look once I finger-slick it back. Ready for prime time.

As soon as I re-emerge, Amber is all over me again.

"Harris, you goose! Where have you been? They're ready for the interview."

Expecting me to follow, she bounces back into the auditorium. Of course I do.

Amber is a revelation. The sweetest human being I've ever met, without contest. Her joy is almost blinding, like looking directly into the sun.

I think I've been spending too much time in the dark.

11

Cleo

My condo is stifling tonight. I'm proud of this place. I worked hard for it, but right now it feels like the walls are closing in.

Three unbearable days have passed since I shared the evening with Harris in his kitchen. It was the greatest night of my life in fifteen long years. We connected. He confided in me. I knew it was the beginning of our new life together.

But I haven't heard from him since.

My phone is in my hand again, for the hundredth time since I got home from work. Everything in my body screams for me to contact him. Text, call, or just show up at his place again.

But why should I have to do all the work? I found him in the hospital, I arranged dinner with my sister, and I met him at his house. It's starting to feel like he's taking me for granted already. Well, I won't have it.

Just as I'm about to text him, something on the television distracts me. God only knows why I still switch on the irrelevant, outdated evening news program every night just to ignore it, but I do. Habit, I guess. But tonight I'm glad.

Harris is on.

I sink into the couch, glued to the TV screen. His hair is slicked back. With sweat? His shirt collar is open and he's flashing that smile. The one that makes my breath catch in my chest. My hand flies to my mouth as I lean forward to be closer to my man. My Harris.

His familiar deep voice is talking about the inspiring work they're doing at this free women's clinic. Apparently, he volunteered there today. If only I'd known, I would have volunteered myself. I wonder if there's some way I can get my hands on his campaign schedule.

The segment is obviously more of a publicity opportunity rather than an actual news story, but I don't care. I'll watch Harris do anything. Anytime, anywhere. Twenty-four hours a day if I could.

Something about Harris is different from his usual public appearances, though. Nobody else could tell, but I notice everything when it comes to him.

He's gleaming. From the inside. He looks genuinely happy and relaxed, the way he did at dinner with Thalia's family.

The reporter-girl beckons to someone off-screen. And then she appears. Bubbly blonde Barbie.

She brags about her charity just long enough to make me sick, then starts in on how "amazing" Harris is and how hard he works. She puts her hand on his shoulder, and he grins at her like a lovesick moron.

And just like that, the segment is over.

My mouth hangs open. I'm incredulous. I can't believe what I just saw.

Obviously, Harris is cheating on me.

With that silly blonde girl. She's so young, she barely looks legal. Is that why he hasn't called me in three days?

Without thinking, I slam my phone down on the coffee table.

Then I storm into the kitchen and pour myself a glass of wine. Standing over the sink, I down it, then pour another. This can't happen. Harris is mine, and I won't let anyone take him from me this time.

Courage up and inhibitions down, I go for my phone. The screen is cracked now, just like the cracks forming in my liaison with Harris.

Screens can be fixed, and so can affairs.

I text Harris, inviting myself back to his house for the weekend. If I can recreate that perfect moment at the kitchen table, he'll forget all about the blonde and our relationship will be back on track.

He doesn't respond immediately, so I decide another glass of wine won't hurt.

I text him again.

Finish the bottle.

Text again.

While I lie on the couch waiting for his response, I replay the news segment in my mind. Over and over again. What is that look? The one he gives to other women, but never to me?

Another hour goes by. Still nothing from Harris.

The ache in my heart expands, filling my body with a blackness that can only be banished by his touch.

I need him.

Again, I text. And again. I don't know how many times, but enough that he won't be able to ignore me.

Mentally drained, I lie down again, clutching my phone. This inanimate black screen feels like my only lifeline to

Harris right now. Wherever he is, he's on the other end of it, and if he would put forward a tiny bit of effort, we could re-connect any second.

He would remember that I'm the only woman for him. Always have been.

I'm clinging to that hope, but I feel like I'm drowning. I can't get the picture of him mooning over that girl out of my mind. I want to cry, but I can't. My eyes haven't been wet in a decade.

12

Harris

My arms ache after lugging around what seems like thousands of pounds of metal today. I'm grateful to be home. Tomorrow is another full day of campaigning, which will require waking before dawn. I hope I can survive a few more weeks of this grueling schedule.

I wander into my kitchen, which hasn't felt the same since Cleo was here. This room was functional. Neat, clean, and spare. But she left something behind. Energy? Spirit? Whatever it is, the room pulsates with it even though she's gone.

But Cleo is the last person I want to think about tonight. So I pour myself a glass of bourbon and carry it down the hall. I enter my home office and relax into my leather desk chair, swirling the bourbon and inhaling its aroma. As I sip, I close my eyes and go back over the day.

Being with Amber was like an awakening. She was so open, so friendly. So loving. The warmth of her presence reminded me how lonely I've become. How very alone I am on a daily basis.

To protect myself, I've pushed away every woman who's ever tried to get close to me. Which has left me empty and despondent. A would-be politician with a counterfeit smile, drinking and sleeping alone. Three weeks from what is supposed to be my big day, and I have no one meaningful to share it with.

I swig the rest of my bourbon and return the glass to the kitchen. The lights are out, allowing me to peer through the window into the night. Flashes of women come into my mind, confusing and confounding me. What do I want? *Who* do I want?

One thing has become clear to me today, though. Allowing Cleo back into my life was a mistake. Over the last twenty-four hours she's sent me an endless stream of texts, the most significant of which informed me that she was dating some student of hers but has now broken up with him. In order to "clear the way" for us to be together. Her exact words. She's attempting to claim me as her territory, as if my consent is irrelevant.

This campaign has been far more stressful than I expected and I'm in the final stretch. I can't deal with her, too. If she was more predictable, calmer, it might work. But then she wouldn't be Cleo.

She wants to come to the house again this weekend.

I pick up my phone and text her.

No.

If I'm going to disrupt my schedule by bringing a woman into my life, it's because I invited her. I can't be taken advantage of.

I set my alarm for tomorrow's ridiculous wake-up time and settle in to bed. But I can't sleep. Something is keeping me awake. Or rather, someone.

I fight it for far too long, then give in to the temptation and text her, too.

2 Weeks Before Election Day

13

Cleo

Harris has more guts than I gave him credit for. He actually told me not to come to his house this weekend.

Given, I did make a nuisance of myself texting him no fewer than eight times last night. Blame it on the wine. He claims not to have time to see me now, due to the campaign. He's probably lying just to get rid of me, so he can get with that sickeningly cute blonde.

But none of that matters. So what if he's taken by some girl's superficial charms temporarily? I'm the one who's going to last.

Now all I need is a plan. There's no way I'm going to sit back and wait for her to disappear. I need to be proactive, and the sooner the better. The first thing to do is find who that little woman is. They said her name on the news report last night, but I paid her zero attention until after I saw Harris slobber all over her. I don't even know what her stupid charity is.

I pull out my laptop and go to the local news website. After a minute or two of searching, I find the story.

Women's Wellness Center of Washington is the duller-than-dull name of the charity. The actual name of the tiny princess who founded it is Amber Lindstrom. A spoiled rich girl, obviously. People with normal backgrounds don't start charities when they're twenty-two. Undoubtedly, her father is wealthy and she knows nothing about real hardship.

I'd like to think Harris is smarter than to be taken by such a shallow human being, but I have to face the facts. Harris is wealthy, too. Amber is probably just his type. Pretty, polite, and polished. The perfect political wife, something I could never be.

But moping about it isn't my style.

On the Wellness Center's website, I go to the "Volunteer" page. Above the photo of Amber and the underprivileged women she's using as props is the information I was hoping to find.

"If you'd like to make a difference in your community, become a volunteer for the Women's Wellness Center of Washington," it says. "Opportunities are always available to gain valuable experience and be a part of helping women in need."

It just so happens that I'm a woman in need myself. In need of one thing: Harris Cox.

Lucky for me, I just so happen to be free for a couple hours in the afternoon tomorrow. But I need someone to volunteer with me. If I go alone, and god forbid Harris shows up again, the whole thing will look far too suspicious.

I'll get Thalia to go with me.

I find the address and phone number of the Wellness Center and enter them into my phone.

Princess Amber will be receiving a visit from the Tait sisters tomorrow. I hope she's prepared.

14

Thalia

I don't know why I've never noticed how Warren leans over the table so close to his plate when he eats. He's shoveling salad into his mouth, his face two inches from the food. It's disgusting. He's like a dog eating his chow, crunching the too-big croutons with an open mouth.

I didn't want to spend the money, but he insisted on taking me out to dinner at another restaurant in town. For research, he says. Of course, he ordered the surf and turf, the most expensive dish on the menu. I ordered a bowl of chili. This is how it goes. I scrimp and save every penny to make sure the mortgage is paid, while he buys whatever he likes, all the while the restaurant is failing. He doesn't even know that Cleo just bailed us out. We'd be on the brink of foreclosure and headed for actual homelessness if it wasn't for my sister.

Warren's always been focused on his goals. His ambition was one of the things that attracted me to him when we first met. But lately all the problems with the restaurant have changed him. I suppose they've changed me, too. The stress has me so bogged down, trying to manage the household and make ends meet when we're heading full-speed toward financial disaster. I used to be light-hearted, happy, and fun. I miss the youthful woman I used to be, and I'd do anything to get her back. Now I feel like a sad old hag, lines on my face and bags under my eyes. Even my once-bouncy curls have begun to droop.

I don't think Warren has even noticed.

"So," he says between forkfuls of salad, "the new dishes are supposed to be delivered tomorrow. It's going to make the place much more hip, bring in the younger crowd."

"New dishes?"

"Yeah, don't tell me you forgot. We're getting all new dishes for the restaurant." Crunch, crunch, croutons.

"So a new menu, then?"

He laughs, and I can see the crouton bits in his mouth. "No, not those kinds of dishes. You know, plates, bowls, mugs..."

"You're going to bring in more customers with new plates?"

Swig of soda. Gulp. "Yeah. They're orange. Very hip."

I can't speak. There is nothing left to say to this man. As usual, he doesn't notice my silence.

Just as he's finishing the last merciful bite of salad, the waitress delivers Warren's huge steak and lobster tail and my chili with saltines. He saws away at the overcooked steak. He always orders it well done to the point of being inedible. No wonder the restaurant is failing.

"I've been thinking, Thal," he says. I hold back the sarcastic comment that springs to mind. "You know what we need? A good vacation, just the two of us. A real swanky resort for a week. Or maybe even a cruise. We deserve it."

My general annoyance with him levels up past mild irritation and moderate anger, topping out at complete rage. "Who would take care of the girls? And more importantly, how could we possibly pay for that? There is no money, Warren. We are broke."

He looks up from his sawing, with an infuriating blankness. "I told you, I'm going to be bringing new customers to the restaurant real soon. We're going to be rolling in cash before you know it. Promise." He winks without smiling, then goes back to his butchery.

"I'm sick of your broken promises, Warren. Why don't you face the fact that your restaurant has failed? It's not working, and you don't know how to fix it."

He puts down the knife and fork for a second. An unexpected stillness falls over the table. "Are you calling me a failure?" he asks.

"I'm asking you to admit the truth. Get a job, Warren. Just sell the restaurant, cut your losses or whatever you have to do, and go back to driving trucks. Please. I'm tired."

He surprises me by not immediately defending himself. He appears to actually think for a minute before speaking. "One more month, okay? Can you give me one more month?" he asks.

"And then if it's not working, you'll close it and get a job?"

"Yes, I'll go back to trucking if that's what you want. I promise."

I feel my shoulders lower and my jaw muscles unclench. I didn't realize how much tension I've been carrying. Past experience has taught me to be cautious with believing Warren's promises, but at this point, it's better than nothing. My stomach growls, and I dig into my chili, which has just cooled to a safe temperature.

As I'm swallowing my first mouthful, my phone buzzes in my purse. Warren hates when I check my phone at dinner, so I apologize, reach into my bag, and pretend to turn it off, sneaking a glance at the incoming text first.

After an hour of him smacking his food and rambling on about his grandiose plans, we head home. Once there, he spends his predictable half hour grunting in the bathroom, and I dash off a nervous response to the text from earlier. I undress and get into bed, waiting for Warren to come in for our nightly routine. As usual, I lay there staring at the ceiling while he pounds me for about four minutes, groans, then rolls over and falls asleep.

15

Cleo

"This was the best idea, Cleo," says Thalia as I pull up in front of the Wellness Center. The little white building is all clean lines and potted bamboo. Sleek and modern, while still managing to feel approachable. If Amber designed this, she's good.

"I thought we should, you know, give back…" I say, too disingenuous to convince even myself. "Since we know what it's like to be in need."

Thalia throws her arms around my neck as I put the parking brake on. She actually believes that's why we're here. Apparently, I've gotten very good at lying. So good that even the person who knows me the best can't tell. I'm not sure whether I should be proud of that or not.

As she pulls away, I notice she's not wearing her wedding ring. Troubles with Warren must be getting serious.

We cross the damp parking lot to the front door, sidestepping the ever-present puddles. Before I can even touch the handle, the door is thrown open from the inside by a very exuberant woman.

It's Amber, in the flesh.

"You must be Cleo and Thalia!" she beams. Her smile is so perfect I want to hate it. "Come on in. I'm so happy you're here."

The lobby is bright and breezy. Clean white walls and a pine floor, accented with colorful graphic art on the walls. I expected this place to be dingy and stale-smelling, but it feels upscale and sophisticated. Against my will, I'm impressed.

Thalia and I really do know what it's like to need help. I don't want to remember, but I do. Unpleasant memories of childhood force their way into my consciousness. The image of Thalia crying over my mother as she lay passed out on the floor makes me sick. If a lovely, sweet lady like Amber had been there to help us, things could have been different.

I'm so caught up in my reverie that I don't even realize I've drifted down the hall behind Amber and Thalia. What am I thinking? These wretched memories serve me no purpose, so I push them back down to the abyss from which they came.

I must focus on the present.

Amber directs us into a room with a large executive conference table. On it are a bunch of file boxes which contain pre-folded donation request letters, and some other boxes full of pre-printed envelopes. Thalia and I take a seat. Amber shows us how to stuff the envelopes.

"No need to seal or stamp them," she says. "The machine will do that."

She flashes that engaging smile again, and I find myself smiling back. I don't smile at anybody unless I want something.

I'm afraid I like her.

"I know it's a simple task, but we rely on human hands for this part. We really appreciate you. I can't thank you enough for helping out."

"You're so welcome," says Thalia. I smile silently again.

I disappoint myself.

Amber sweeps out of the room with a promise to come check on us in a little while. So far, this mission is a complete bust. All I've done is confirm that Harris is right to choose Amber instead of me. She's selfless, kind, and warm. And worst of all, genuinely happy. All things which I am not.

Should I just give up right now? Stuff these envelopes and go home in defeat?

Impossible. I know myself better than that. I can't drive past Harris Cox signs all over Seattle and just ignore the fact that I've lost him all over again. The fire inside flames up with a vengeance.

I grab a stack of envelopes and jam the letters inside as fast as I can. All I want is to finish this job and get far, far away from the perfect princess Amber. I find a rhythm.

Grab envelope, grab letter, shove inside, toss in pile.

Grab envelope, grab letter, shove inside, toss in pile.

"Cleo!" Thalia grabs my arm. I stop mid-shove. "Cleo, what's going on? Slow down, you're scrunching all the paper!"

I close my eyes and shake my head. "Sorry. I don't do administrative work. I'll try to be more delicate."

Thalia stares at me longer than she needs to, but decides not to ask any more questions. We both get back to work stuffing envelopes. After a few minutes of working in silence, she opens a conversation I wasn't expecting.

"Did you ever talk to Harris about doing dinner again?"

Of course I didn't. I wanted him alone, and I got him

that way. But that's not information I'm ready to share, so instead I say, "You mean the Warren-less dinner?"

Thalia giggles. "Yeah, the Warren-less one."

"No, I haven't really had time." The lamest excuse in the world. Everyone has time for exactly what they want to do. But time is the perfect scapegoat, because no one ever argues.

"That's okay, don't worry about it," she says. "He's busy now, anyway."

I raise an eyebrow.

"I mean with the campaign. Right?" she says.

The door cracks open, and Amber's blue eyes peek into the room.

"I'm so sorry to interrupt you lovely ladies, but I wondered if you'd like to take a break? The coffee shop next door makes a mean latte, and I'd love to get to know you both a little better."

Suddenly my fire is lit again. Yes, this is just what I need to get back on track. The whole point of this afternoon is to figure Amber out. Find her weakness, get under her skin, and use that to wedge her away from Harris.

"Took the words right out of my mouth," I say. This time, my smile is more of a smirk. The way I like it.

Halfway through my caffè breve, I'm about to give up. This girl is so sweet they could throw away all the sugar in the coffee shop. Just sweeten all the drinks with her smile. It's nauseating. She doesn't have a single fault. And she's clearly hiding her relationship with Harris. I've launched all my conversational ammunition at her, trying to get her off-balance, to no avail. I'm exhausted, but I still have one more round in the chamber.

"Amber," I say between sips. "Do you have a boyfriend? Tell us all the spicy details." The fake girl-bonding thing is too easy.

She smiles again and actually blushes this time. "I wasn't going to say anything since it's early, but... yeah, I just started seeing a new guy. He's pretty amazing."

Thalia's eyes light up. She loves this kind of thing. "Oooh, what's his name?" I silently thank her for saving me the trouble of asking.

"I don't want to say just yet. It's still so new."

Thalia nods knowingly. "Don't want to jinx it."

Amber laughs. "Exactly!"

They're both giggling like sisters now. I regret everything about this day.

Amber touches my hand and asks me, "What about you, Cleo? You're so gorgeous. You probably have a ton of guys all the time."

Thalia gives me the eye. She's never approved of the fact that for over a decade, that statement has absolutely been true.

"Guilty as charged," I say.

Amber laughs again. It tinkles this time. How does her laugh manage to sound like wind chimes?

"So no one special in your life? I bet there's a guy who would kill to have you all to himself," she says.

"Well... since you asked..." I say. I wasn't going to go this route, but she opened the door and I'm going to walk through it. "I do have someone."

Thalia's eyebrows go up, so high I think they might shoot off her forehead.

"Even my dear sister doesn't know about him."

"Juicy!" says Amber. She leans forward, sipping her latte.

"Let's play a game," I say. "I'll tell you—"

But before I can make my proposal, a tall, handsome

man in a long, wool coat comes up behind Thalia. He places a hand on her shoulder and says, "Excuse me, ladies. I don't mean to interrupt."

Amber glows at him and chirps, "James! You're back!" She hops to her feet and hugs him. "Ladies," she says. "This is James Thatcher. He owns the photography gallery a few doors down. He's been on a photo tour to... Where? Paris?"

The corners of James's mouth turn up just enough to confirm. Evidently a man of few words. Amber introduces Thalia and me with enough enthusiasm to fool anyone into thinking we're all lifelong friends. James nods at me and I nod back. With Thalia, though, he lingers. Looks into her eyes a little deeper than necessary. Touches her shoulder again. She blushes.

"Enchantée, Ladies," he says. But the greeting is directed at Thalia, not me. He reaches into his breast pocket, pulls out a business card, and slips it into Thalia's hand. "I'd be delighted to have you as a guest at the gallery."

He nods again, and he's off. Thalia's eyes go wide and she stashes the card in her purse. I don't care that she was the subject of Monsieur Charming's attention. I have information to get. I steer the conversation right back to where it was before he came on the scene.

"So now for my game," I say. "I'll tell you one thing about my man, Amber, and you tell one thing about yours." I'm the only one who knows we're both talking about Harris. This is the perfect way to find out how serious he is about her.

"You're on!" she says. "You first."

I decide to ease my way into this. "He once took me on the perfect date. A picnic in the mountains."

"Super romantic!" Amber gushes. "My guy secretly

asked my dad what my favorite flower was, then brought me a whole bouquet on our first date."

Thalia's hand flies to her heart. "So thoughtful!"

"I know, he—"

"My turn!" I say, too sternly. I take a breath and calm myself. "My man shares his deepest, darkest secrets with me. And *only* me."

"I love that," says Amber, breathless. "Okay, um, my guy just made a huge donation to the Center. Anonymously."

I fight the urge to roll my eyes. Money means nothing to Harris and his family. Well, that's not exactly accurate. Money means influence, which is what he is obviously buying with Amber.

"My man is utterly incapable of living without me. I am everything to him. And if any woman ever, *ever* tries to come between us, she will find herself at the other end of a wrath so violent she will never recover."

Amber almost chokes on her coffee. My eyes bore into hers, making sure she understands exactly what I'm saying. Her eyelids flutter. She swallows and looks down at the table.

"Your relationship sounds... intense. I'm happy for you."

I'm pretty sure she won't be messing around with Harris anymore after this. But I won't take any chances.

We go back to the office and finish stuffing envelopes. But before we drive away, I leave a little something behind.

16

Cleo

He knocks on my office door. I already know who it is, because I invited him here. I sit on the front of my desk, cross my legs, and say, "Come in."

The door opens, and there he is. Looking as sexy as always. Maybe a little confused, but who could blame him?

"Hello, Ryan," I say. He closes the door behind him and surveys the situation. I can tell he's more than a little surprised to see me with my blouse halfway-unbuttoned and my skirt hiked up. I bite my lip and cock my head. "Have you missed me?"

He rushes me, not bothering with an answer, and buries my mouth in his. His hands slide to my waist, and I lock my legs around him. This is what we're good at, and it's been too long. When I broke up with him, I meant it. But I called him this morning because I need his help with something. I figure I might as well give before I receive.

When we're finished, he tries to stroke my cheek. I don't want him to get the wrong idea, so I push his hand down.

Gently, though. I don't want to alienate him, either.

"I'm so glad you've changed your mind about us," he says. "We're good together, Cleo."

"You're good, Ryan." It's true what they say. Flattery will get you everywhere.

As I button my blouse, I get to the point of why I called him here. "Ryan, do you believe in destiny?"

"I'd like to," he says. "I mean, everybody wants to think there's a point to this whole thing, don't they?"

"Yes..." I try again. "Do you believe that some people are just destined to be together?"

"Umm, I'd like to say yes," he says. He looks hopeful. He thinks I'm talking about us, which is exactly what I want.

"Good. Well, sometimes people are destined to be together, but then someone else gets in the way. A third party, if you will."

Ryan nods his head. He's following me, just the way I want him to. I continue.

"And then that third party needs to be removed. Only once that person is gone can destiny move forward and be fulfilled. Do you understand what I'm saying?"

He nods his head again.

"There's a third party that needs to be removed, and I need your help to do it."

"Anything, Cleo." Always so eager.

"Then come with me. I can't explain just yet, so you'll have to trust me."

Minutes later, Ryan is in the passenger seat of my car and we're heading to Princess Amber's Women's Wellness Center. I'm taking a risk being seen out in public with a student, but at this point I couldn't care less. I will wedge Harris away from Amber if it's the last thing I do. If it costs me my job, so be it. It won't matter because I'll be

Harris's wife.

Ryan questions me the whole car ride, because I haven't told him where we're going or what we're doing. There are two parts to my plan, and he will have to execute them both perfectly. When we're in the parking lot, I finally give him his orders.

"You're sure this is what you want?" he says.

I place one hand on his knee and slowly run it up toward his thigh. "Oh, I'm sure," I purr. "You will do it… for me?"

He leans in to kiss me, but I place a finger on his lips and shake my head. "Later. Let's go inside."

Just like last time, Amber throws the door open before I can even grab the handle. "Cleo! You're back! I didn't know you were volunteering again."

"Sorry, no, not today. I dropped by because I'm pretty sure I left my phone here. Do you have a Lost and Found?"

Amber sweeps the two of us into the lobby. "Yes, of course! I'm so glad you came by. It's right here." She reaches under the front desk. "I wasn't sure if it was yours or your sister's. So many people come through here every day it's hard to know."

She hands me my phone and I turn it on. "Don't let me be rude," I say. "Amber, this is my student from the university, Ryan. He's considering volunteering, isn't that right?"

He dutifully nods his head.

"Oh, super!" she says.

"Ryan, this is Amber. She runs this wonderful institution."

By the time they finish shaking hands, my phone is all fired up. "Hey, do you two mind if I take a photo of you? My camera's been a little screwy and I just want to make sure it's working again."

"Sure!" says Amber. If I looked like her, I'd probably want my picture taken all the time. She throws her arm around Ryan and I steel myself against that engaging smile.

"One, two, three!" On cue, Ryan wraps his arms around her waist, pulls Amber close, and kisses her full on the lips just as I take the photo. Amber's palms fly up to Ryan's shoulders to push him away, but he keeps a tight grip. He checks me out of the corner of his eye, and when he sees that I've got the photo, he lets her go. She stumbles backward, her eyes wide and her hands shaking.

If some guy did that to me, I would slap him across the face, but she's far too well-mannered for that. She pulls a tissue out of the box on the desk and wipes her lips. "Ummm…" He's actually rendered her speechless. And smile-less.

"Ryan, how dare you," I say. "Apologize to poor Amber this minute."

I enclose Amber's hand in both of mine. "I'm so sorry about Ryan. I think he might be…" I whisper in her ear, as if we're close girlfriends. "…on the spectrum. He has difficulty with impulse control." Complete lies, but Amber buys them. She looks at him with genuine sympathy.

"No harm done," she says. Her smile is back, and she's bright as sunshine again. "Oh, except that photo. Cleo, can you delete it?"

I make a show of looking at my phone. Ryan and Amber liplocked in what appears to be red-hot passion is burning up my screen. It's so perfect I have to suppress the smirk that's pulling at the corners of my mouth. Immediately, I close the photo and turn my screen around to show Amber the giant crack in it.

"Turns out my camera's still not working. The picture

didn't even take. Thank goodness." Amber's shoulders relax as she clearly believes my story. I'm continually surprised at how easy it is to fool people. "I'll just borrow your bathroom before we go, if you don't mind."

Amber nods her head and I make my way down the hall, leaving Ryan alone with her. Now for part two of the plan. In the car, I instructed Ryan to apologize profusely to Amber the second I was out of sight. I told him to make up whatever story he wanted to excuse his behavior, as long as it took him a good several minutes to tell it.

In the meantime, I sneak into Amber's office. The girl is so trusting she leaves the door propped wide open all day long.

I'm expecting Ryan to keep her occupied for a few minutes, but I can't waste any time. Just as I'd hoped, her computer isn't password protected. I open the browser and go straight to Twitter. She's left her account logged in, as I suspected she would. Blind trust is a really stupid trait.

Now to pull Amber's strings as if she's my little marionette. With my help, she's about to impugn Harris's character on the internet. He'll never trust her sweet, sweet self again.

I lean over the keyboard and type a furious tweet storm.

"I regret to announce that the Women's Wellness Center of Washington withdraws its endorsement of Harris Cox for Congress. Mr. Cox recently volunteered at the Center. While initially we were appreciative of his efforts, some unfortunate comments have since come to light. No further details can be shared at the present time, but suffice it to say that the women of Seattle deserve a representative who respects them. We wish Mr. Cox the best. However, we do wish that his best could be better."

Reading it over, I'm satisfied. It sounds like a professional public statement made by an institution. The classic formula. Make some vague accusations not backed up by facts and let the public read into it what they will.

Harris will never have anything to do with her again.

But just before I publish the whole thread, I realize I'm about to make an inexcusably stupid mistake. I can't publish this. Amber will see it, know that she didn't type it, and she'll figure out it was me. I'm the only one who had the opportunity to sneak into her Twitter account while she was out of her office.

And guaranteed she'll tell Harris. What an idiot move.

Luckily, I delete all the tweets before I make the biggest mistake of my life. Now I have to come up with something on the fly. Ryan is still talking to Amber in the lobby, but I'm out of time. You can only pretend to be in the bathroom for so long.

An idea sparks in my head. I need to tweet something she'd *want* to deny. So when she does deny it, everyone will assume she's lying.

On impulse, I type, "Harris Cox is a jackass." Would Amber use that word? Anything else that comes to mind seems too naughty for the pretty princess. Jackass it is.

"He's a dirty skirt chaser with no respect for women."

That's it. That's all I have time to type. Sounds mawkish and immature, but I imagine that's how Amber would write. Hopefully, it's enough to anger Harris and keep him away from her for good.

I duck into the bathroom, flush the toilet, run the faucet for a few seconds, then stride down the hallway to the lobby. Ryan and Amber seem to be just finishing up their conversation. I almost feel bad for tricking Ryan into being my accomplice. Almost.

"Thanks for waiting," I smile. "Well, I guess we'd better

let Amber get back to her important work. Thank you sooo much for all you do."

Amber takes my hand. "No, Cleo, thank you for volunteering. I'm truly grateful."

I pull Ryan out the door and don't look back. If all goes according to plan, I'll never have to see that woman again.

17

Harris

I've spent most of my adult life alone. My father is usually away on business, and my mother is always at the hospital. Well, technically, she's my stepmother. My real mother died when I was two years old. I have no memories of her, but the few photos I've saved tell me everything I need to know. The way her smile beamed, the warmth she exuded when she held me on her lap... Her love for me was perfect, and I've never been able to replace it.

When Cleo and I separated after the accident, I was inconsolable for a while. Though she couldn't fill the hole that the loss of my mother left behind, she gave me focus. She was such an intense presence that she almost took over my life, which was fine with me. No one had ever cared as much for me as Cleo did.

And then my father took her away.

Once a few months had passed, I realized I would have to move on, because a future with Cleo was forbidden. I deluded myself into thinking that replacing her would be easy. After all, Cleo practically fell into my lap in college. What a fool I was.

I never had more than one date with any other woman. My stutter gave me anxiety, but that wasn't the problem. I would work up the courage to ask a woman to dinner. We'd have a perfectly nice evening, and I would end the night vowing I'd never be that bored again.

And so I've always been single. Since I bought my first house, I've lived alone. Not even a cat or a dog.

Rumors abound, but none of them are true. I'm neither gay, nor an addict, nor emotionally unavailable.

I'm searching.

Until now, I always thought that I needed a woman as reckless as Cleo. As passionate, driven, and daring.

But I was wrong.

Quite by accident, I've met someone who has changed everything. She's warm, loving, happy, and stable. Nothing like Cleo.

The irony of comparing this glowing, selfless woman to Cleo, while claiming I've moved on from her, is not lost on me.

Deep down, I'm trying to believe that if I ignore Cleo and focus my attentions elsewhere, I'll stop loving her.

Deep down, I also know I won't.

But that won't stop me from trying.

18

Cleo

The sun is waking up, painting the horizon behind the Seattle skyline pink and orange. Finally.

The front seat of my car is getting cramped since I've been sitting in it, parked in front of Harris's house, since it was still dark outside. If Harris doesn't come out soon, I'll probably lose my mind and go break in the front door.

I wish I didn't have to stalk him like this, but he's ignored all my texts and calls. He's left me no choice.

To pass a little more time, I check the Wellness Center's Twitter feed on my phone one more time. I've had my eye on it constantly since yesterday. In the first few hours after Ryan and I left, people were commenting things like, "Has this account been hacked?" and "Amber, you okay? This doesn't sound like you." I was mildly worried Amber would figure out what I'd done, but worse than that, I was disappointed. Bitterly.

No one believed that Amber had actually written the crude messages about Harris. Which means that half of my plan to wrench her away from him had failed. If strangers on the internet didn't believe it was her, neither would he.

But I still have the most volatile ammunition. The photo I took of her and Ryan kissing.

My pre-dawn latte has long since gone cold, but I chug the last of it down, anyway. I can't wait any longer. I get out of my car, straighten my shoulders, and march up the walk to Harris's front door. Phone in hand, I punch the doorbell. Rise and shine, Harris.

I question myself a million ways as I wait for him to come to the door.

Is he even here? Have I wasted the last hour sitting in front of his house after he's already gone? What if he didn't even sleep here last night? What if he spent the night with Amber?

In my mind, a picture forms of Harris cradling Amber in his arms, stroking her golden hair, whispering in her ear. I feel my teeth clamp down and my breath turn shallow. I have to get them apart. He's mine.

Mine.

All mine.

I spin on my heel to storm back to my car. If I knew where Amber lived… She's lucky I don't.

Then I hear a click. I stop and turn around.

The door opens and there is Harris. My body goes limp at the sight of him. He's wearing a tailored black suit with a crisp white shirt. The collar is unbuttoned and his hair is still damp. A little wave hangs over his forehead. I want to wrap it around my finger as I brush my lips all over his neck.

"Cleo? What are you doing here?" He sounds a little clipped.

I peer around him into the house. "Is anyone else here?"

I ask.

Harris shifts his weight and puts a hand up on the door jamb. "No. Why?"

"I, um… I have something I need to show you." I pull my fingers through my hair and wait for him to say something. He doesn't. "Aren't you going to invite me in?"

He shakes his head. No.

"I've got a big day today, Cleo. Whatever it is will have to wait." His voice is firm, but he doesn't close the door. It feels to me like a sign to keep going.

I venture closer to him. Close enough to smell him. To look deep into those troubled eyes.

He looks into mine, too, and we share a moment. Just when I think he's going to take me in his arms, he looks down.

"You have something to show me?" he asks, his voice gentler this time.

"I saw you on television the other night. At the Women's Wellness Center?"

His eyebrows crumple into a scowl, though his mouth remains neutral. I'm surprised to find that lying to Harris is more difficult than lying to anyone else. I take a deep breath and continue.

"I was so inspired by your segment, by their mission… that I just had to help out." His eyebrows go up as his head tilts down. "To volunteer. To help the less fortunate."

He clears his throat. Looks at his watch. "This is certainly a new side of you, Cleo. I'm impressed. But I really do have a schedule to keep today."

"I know, I know," I say. I've got to get this out before it's too late. "The adorable little gal who runs the place—"

"Amber," he cuts in. The way he says her name, like honey dripping from a spoon. It makes me want to find her and scratch her pretty blue eyes out. Instead, I smile bigger than ever.

"Yes. Amber. Well, it turns out... She's not exactly..." Something happens to me around Harris. I planned out what I was going to say down to the very word, but his gaze disarms me. I'm overcome with timidity.

Harris sighs and drops his arm from the door jamb. He's losing patience with me. Enough with the explanations. I'll just show him.

I hold up my phone with the picture of Amber and Ryan kissing in the lobby of the Wellness Center.

But if I expected him to recoil in horror or seethe with rage, I am sorely disappointed. He takes the phone out of my hand, looks closely at the photo, and hands it back to me. His face is the picture of composure, his expression unreadable. Always the professional politician.

"Send her my congratulations. I won't be seeing her again."

Warmth spreads through my body as I realize I've accomplished my mission, despite my bumbling. I want to kiss Harris, to drive with him to all his campaign stops today, to plan another date. But I won't push it. We have time for all that, now that the perky blonde will be out of the picture.

I say, "Good luck today, Harris." And leave it at that.

7 Days Before Election Day

19

Thalia

Before he leaves for work, Warren pauses by the front door. He pulls me toward him and wraps me in a big, firm bear hug that lifts me off my feet. It's a sweet gesture that he's never failed to perform since we were married. Back when going to work meant being on the road in his truck for two or three weeks at a time, those bear hugs meant a lot. But it seems like overkill when I know he'll be back tonight.

While I once cherished these moments, all I want now is to get his hot breath out of my ear. When he unhands me, I peck him on the lips and send him on his way to the restaurant.

I close the door behind him and sag against it, listening as his car rumbles off down the street.

Relief floods my body as I look forward to the hours without my husband. Our daughters are already at school, so I will have the house to myself, as usual. This is not as appealing as it would seem to be. I force myself away from the front door and get to work.

First things first, I clean the kitchen and rinse Warren's breakfast dishes. He always sleeps and eats late because of his hours at the restaurant. After that's done, I busy myself with two loads of laundry. One for the girls and me and one for Warren's work clothes. They have to be washed separately because they always reek of grease.

I putter away the girls' toys and books, then get out a bucket to mop the floors, as I do every day. I wedge the bucket under the faucet in the kitchen sink and turn on the water. As it fills, I find myself staring at nothing, pondering what my life has become. A potpourri of dirty dishes, dirty clothes, and dirty floors. Day after day, the filth redeposits itself. I spend my hours scouring it away, knowing a new layer will reemerge tomorrow.

I wonder why it matters. Maybe it doesn't.

Maybe I don't matter.

The drip of the water overflowing the bucket interrupts my pity party. I hurriedly crank the faucet to off. Some of the water has spilled over onto the kitchen floor, but I don't care. I pour in the liquid floor cleaner, mix it around, and place the bucket on the floor.

I dip, wring, and mop in a perfect rhythm. I've done this thousands of times. I'll do it thousands more.

No one ever thanks me for it.

I notice the wedding ring on my left hand as it grips the mop handle. I prop the mop against the counter so it won't fall over, then twist off the ring. I've taken to removing it every morning after Warren leaves. It goes on again before he comes home at night, but having my ring finger naked all day gives me a sense of freedom I've come to value.

At the coffee shop last week with Cleo, I was so grateful I wasn't wearing it. When James approached our table, there was no mistaking the fact that I was the object of his attention. He never would have dared to give me his phone number if he thought I was married.

I would tell myself there's no harm in a little flirtation with a highly eligible bachelor, but I know what a lie that would be. There is plenty of harm to go around. That is, if I allowed myself to get tangled up in an illicit affair.

Which I have already done.

It's wrong. I know it's wrong, but I'm finding it so hard to care.

Warren was my first boyfriend. He and I started dating in high school, and he asked me to marry him before we even graduated. I put him off for a while because I wasn't sure I was ready to settle down so young. When I told Cleo about his proposals, she couldn't believe I'd turned him down. She quizzed me for an hour about him. What kind of man was he? Was he dependable? Did he have a good job? Could he take care of me?

When I told her he was friendly and kind, and that he was planning to become a truck driver as soon as he could get the proper license, she pressured me to marry him.

"I can't take care of you forever, Thal," she'd said. "Don't let him get away."

So I didn't. We got married at eighteen and became instant adults. Playing house was fun at first, but eventually it got lonely. When he would be on the road for weeks at a time, I had nothing to do and no one to talk to. That's when I started the ritualistic house cleaning. It gave me a sense of accomplishment, seeing the place spic and span. It also gave Warren something pleasant to come home to. I was never particularly beautiful or talented, and I became afraid that Warren would seek the company of other women while he was away.

As far as I know, he didn't. But we don't always know people as well as we think we do.

That's the thought I comfort myself with whenever guilt comes on me, hot as the steam from a teapot.

I feel it burning now, flushing my cheeks. I slop some soapy water on the floor and mop with the fury of a... what? Clever metaphors elude me. Or would it be a simile? I don't know. I didn't go to college like Cleo did.

With the fury of a cheating wife. Because that's what I am.

I scrub at a dark spot near the oven. It's been there since we moved into this house. I've never been able to get it out, but for some reason I think today I will. I scour and rub with my mop, but it's no use.

But I'm not giving up. Not today. I may be a cheater, but I'm no quitter.

I get down on my knees with a scouring pad and some abrasive cleanser. Bare knuckles, I scrub and scrub at the stain. No matter what I do, it won't come out.

Finally, I fall back against the cabinet. I don't know how long I've worked at it, but my hair is hanging in my eyes and I'm sweating. I'll have to take another shower before I see him this afternoon.

I close my eyes and try to picture the dashing, handsome man who's miraculously fallen into my life. But I can't keep his face in front of me. It keeps getting replaced with Warren. Soft, chubby Warren with his goofy grin and terrible manners. I shake my head to try and clear it. All that happens is that I hear the sound of my daughters crying. *Our* daughters.

They are the best thing that's ever happened to me. Am I going to jeopardize their happiness to chase after some foolish fantasy of my own? The answer is yes, and I already know that. I've been over it several times in my mind. I've become quite good at justifying this behavior of mine.

It's not fair that I got married so young. I never got to sow my wild oats. Cleo had all the fun while I took on the adult responsibility. The girls will be sad when Warren and I get divorced, but they'll get over it. Kids are resilient, right? Besides, if I remarry, their new stepfather will be a man of means. Their life will be better for it, not worse.

Despite all my skilled rationalization, I feel tears welling up in my eyes. I loved Warren once. I wish I still did. I wish our lives had gone differently. If only his business was successful instead of a failure. If only he would do something worthy of my respect. I want to look up to my husband, but he's fallen too far down.

I choke on a sob and the tears rush to the surface. This time I let them. I sit on the floor, clutching my mop handle, weeping. Mourning the life I never got to have. Grieving the life I'm about to give up.

I'm leaving Warren. I have to.

As soon as I get the courage to tell him.

20

Harris

Cleo thinks she can pull one over on me. That I don't know what game she's playing. I grew up with a politician for a father; I know every game that exists.

I don't know how she got that photo of Amber, but I wasn't going to give her the satisfaction of asking. I had already determined to put Cleo behind me. Having my space invaded by her at dawn only cemented that decision for me. I won't say I wasn't tempted by her, but she's just too unpredictable. She'll never fit into my life.

I've been so distracted thinking about what to do with her. Avoiding her hasn't worked, because when I ignore her constant texts and calls, she responds by showing up at my house. Fortunately, this morning I was alone, but what happens if one day I'm not?

If she catches me with another woman, she will make my life a living hell. This I know to be true.

Tonight is a big night for me. It's the biggest debate of the campaign and there's a lot riding on this. I can't allow Cleo to intrude in any way.

There's only one thing left to do.

I take a deep breath and take out my phone.

My hands shake as I type the message I know I need to send.

"Cleo, I appreciate all you've done for me. You've been an extraordinary part of my life. But my campaign requires my full attention now. I hope you understand."

I send the message, knowing I should have written more. Should have been more explicit. Should have told her to stay away, to leave me alone, or maybe even just block her number altogether.

But somehow I just can't bring myself to do that.

21

Cleo

Harris's final debate before the election is going to start streaming in a few minutes and I want to pay attention, but this anger buzzing in my head is drowning out all outside sounds. I get up and pace irritatedly, without a goal, just burning off negative energy. After everything I've done for him, everything we've been through together, he thinks he can just blow me off.

He's wrong. What he should have done is call me. Ask me to go with him to his debate tonight, give him the support he needs. Who else is going to be there for him? Amber should be ancient history by now. He needs me, even if he doesn't realize it.

After going round the living room of my condo three times, I pick up my phone. No hesitating, I just call his personal number. Only one ring goes by, and I hear "Cleo?"

My voice sticks in my throat for a minute. I'm nervous, which seems to be my new normal around Harris. "I... want to wish you luck." What an inane comment.

"Uh, thanks," he says. I can hear him talking to someone else away from the phone. A woman? It had better not be Amber. To me, he says, "Is there something you need?"

"Do you know where I am right now?"

"Cleo, I don't have time for riddles. My debate's about to start. This will have to wait."

"I'm sitting at home alone, in front of my laptop. I would be there with you, if you'd asked. I haven't heard from you since I showed you that picture of Amber. You're going to have to work on your communication skills if we're going to have a relationship."

"A relationship?" He's talking in a loud whisper, and I can picture him turning away from whomever else was fluttering around him. At least I have his full attention now. "Let me be clear with you, Cleo. What we had fifteen years ago is gone, and whatever you're trying to start now is bad for me and my career." He's raising his voice as if he doesn't care who hears him, and he's almost spitting the words out. Where did this animosity come from? "There is no relationship between you and me. As far as I'm concerned, you're dead to mm-mm-me." The last word gets stuck. It doesn't come out until he forces it out in an awkward burst of effort.

I feel a small triumph at the return of the stutter. It means he's deeply uncomfortable with what he's saying. He doesn't really want to get rid of me, but for some reason, he feels he has to.

"You need me, Harris. You're stuttering again. You're nervous and scared. I could help you with your phobia, give you the support you need. You're not strong enough to do this alone."

"C-Cleo!" He's lost control now. "I have to focus on the campaign. This debate is in-c-credibly important." He's huffing erratically.

"Come see me afterw —"

"No." A pause, as his breathing slows and calms. He says, deliberately, "Do. Not. Call. Me. Again." Then he hangs up the phone.

I can't believe he hung up on me. How dare he?

Seconds later, his website mocks me too, as the moderator comes on smiling, introducing the evening's debate. Harris's polished, professional portrait flashes up on the screen.

Fifteen years I've waited for him, biding my time with tedious, vapid men. He would've been mine already if it hadn't been for that horrible accident and the dead little girl. That damned secret is what's kept us apart. If only he wasn't such a coward. That's why he's trying to reject me now. Weakness and fear.

To hell with that. He's not getting rid of me that easily.

I pour myself a glass of wine and sit down to endure the debate. I can't miss a minute of his career, no matter how furious I am. By the end of the first predictable question, my thoughts start to drift. This man needs me. He thinks I'm a danger to him, but I'll just have to prove that's not true. I'll show him he's safer with me than without.

Avoiding me is worse for him than being with me.

He'll see.

22

Cleo

Like bile leaking into my body, hatred is rising into the back of my throat. Consuming me.

Blind thoughts of sabotage. Punishment. Revenge.

Pounding in my head, Harris's condescending voice echoes over and over and over, taunting me. *"YOU'RE DEAD TO ME. DO NOT CALL ME AGAIN."*

Watching that debate was intolerable. Sixty minutes of his arrogant independence, every smug smile driving the knife of betrayal deeper into my core.

How dare he try to ostracize me? He can't forbid me from being part of his life. We share the inescapable bond of destiny, written in blood on a deserted mountain road fifteen years ago.

Restless, with nowhere to direct my fury, I get up to deposit the empty wine bottle in the kitchen. I can't sit here all night, being eaten alive by bitterness.

How can I make him see he loves me? He needs me. Why should I be the only one to suffer if he's too cowardly to admit it?

Staring blindly into the darkness through the kitchen window, my mind drifts. I reconsider vengeance and ponder coercion. What do I want? Harris the fly, drowned in vinegar or caught in my honey lure...

Nothing comes to me. No brilliant plot of revenge, no irresistible strategy to win back his love.

It's just me, alone, pining angrily after a man who hasn't wanted me for over a decade. I disgust myself.

Despondency descends. I drag down the hallway and collapse on my empty, loveless bed. My barren eyes have no tears. I'm dead inside.

But something won't let me rest. At the base of my spine is a hot, glowing ember urging me back to life. Compelling me to rise, find a solution, fix this.

The flame kindling in my soul, I get to my feet. I will not lie down and die.

23

Harris

Mentally exhausted from the debate, I'm glad to be home after a long day. Normally I'd let my massage shower ease away some of the day's tension, then head right to bed. Campaigning always seems to involve early mornings, even if that just means strategy meetings at the office.

But tonight I'm making an exception.

This is easily the most imprudent decision I've made since I decided to run for public office. It would be fair even to call it stupid. Yet here I am, giving in to the temptation.

It involves a woman, of course. She'll be here any minute.

And I can't wait.

24

Cleo

I shouldn't be doing this, but I can't help myself.

I'm acting on instinct, like a feral cat stalking an unsuspecting wild bird. Harris is my prey, and I'm about to pounce.

My left shoulder smacks against the door frame as I leave my condo to go down to the parking garage. My tires skid on the pavement as I slam on the brakes. The wine from earlier has kicked in and I'm too buzzed to be driving, but I have to get to Harris's house.

Though I try to keep my attention on the road, his voice keeps intruding on my thoughts. He's never going to go away. No matter what I do or where I go, I'll never be free of him.

I'm not going to let him win. Does he really want to turn our epic love affair into a legendary battle for dignity?

That would be the height of stupidity on his part.

Tonight I'm giving him one last chance to decide.

Is he with me or against me?

Taking a deep breath, I've almost arrived at my target. Wary of the narrow, single lane between the parked cars on both sides of the road, I slow the car to a crawl. Fortunately, this placid little avenue is deserted at night. I'm not sure if I'd be able to negotiate sharing the road with an oncoming vehicle in my current condition.

A wave of nausea punches me in the gut. I blame it on the wine because I don't dare second-guess what I'm about to do.

As I approach his house, I hit the brakes, stopping the car in the middle of the street. All the lights are on in the front room. Is he home? I didn't expect him to be back from the debate yet.

Obviously, that was a severe miscalculation. I meant to get here first. To be waiting for him when he arrived. Now what?

I want to focus on making an alternate plan, but I can't keep my mind from reliving the evening I spent with Harris inside that house. How I crave the fulfillment of that titillating conversation we had in the kitchen...

But just as my thoughts are drifting past the filmy gray sheers in the window into Harris's bedroom, I see him. Or more accurately, his silhouette. He's left the heavy draperies open, leaving only the sheer curtains to conceal the inside of the house.

Barely a second goes by before it happens. A woman walks into the room. And kisses him.

Her arms around his neck, his hands on her waist. Tender and slow, he embraces her. Every touch a betrayal.

Like a bomb detonating in my chest, all the love I've ever had for that man dies a blazing, fiery death.

My head clears instantly, and my insides seethe with a fervent need for revenge. Now I know why he rejected me. That timid little coward couldn't handle me, so he replaced me with a pony-tailed whore.

Amber.

I pull a U-turn at the roundabout, heading back the way I came. The plan just changed.

Damn that man. I thought I was everything he wanted. All these years, I assumed he missed me as desperately as I missed him. I wasted my life believing he would have chosen me if he could have.

And now I find out he's getting intimate with another woman.

If I didn't love him so much, I would kill him.

6 Days Before Election Day

25

Harris

"Excuse me, Mr. Cox?" The receptionist in my campaign office (Kellen, I think?) is interrupting me on an early morning phone call with a donor. I wave him away without a word. Alexander Sawyer and his hundreds of thousands of dollars need my attention. Kellen does not. What is that old saying about it being hard to find good help?

I spin my leather chair around backwards to focus on Sawyer's concern. He wants to wrangle a commitment out of me to make an appearance at his daughter's birthday party. I'm trying to decline diplomatically, but I'm distracted by a nervous gulp behind me. "I'm sorry, Mr. Cox, but I'm pretty sure you'll want to see this." Kellen again.

Turning back around in my chair, I motion him in to the office. He drops a manila envelope on the desk in front of me. It's damp, spotted with dirty rain drops. My name is scribbled on the front, but there's no address or postage stamp. This is highly unusual.

A sense of foreboding settles into my chest. Instinctively, I sense this isn't good.

"I'm sorry, Alexander. There's a development that needs my attention right away. I'll get back to you on that invitation. Wish Nia happy birthday for me." I hang up the phone.

"What is this?" My stomach tightens.

"I'm so sorry, Mr. Cox, I didn't mean to interrupt you — I hope I did the right thing — I wasn't sure, it seemed important — I was taking the recycling out, and there was this envelope — I thought it might be trash so I looked inside — I'm sorry, maybe I shouldn't have—"

"Kellen?" He nods. "Get to the point."

He clears his throat. "I found this outside under the back doormat, opened it, and brought it straight to you. Sir."

A bright red flush creeps up his neck and colors his cheeks.

"Did you look inside?" I ask.

He swallows and nods. He's clearly embarrassed by what he's seen.

It hits me. Someone is trying to blackmail me.

"Whatever it is will remain completely confidential. Correct?"

He nods again.

"Thank you, Kellen. I appreciate you bringing this to me directly." He blinks, but doesn't move. "Please. Close the door behind you on your way out."

Like a caged dog who's just been freed, he stands paralyzed for a moment before darting out of my office.

Now I'm alone with this malicious delivery. I close my eyes and take a deep breath. All of my indiscretions flash through my mind, like a twisted funhouse of doom. With just days to go until the election, someone wants revenge. A political rival? An old liaison? Or a current one?

Oh God, I don't want to know what's in here.

I swallow hard and pull out the contents: a single sheet of paper. It's a photocopy of an old newspaper article, with the headline that's seared into my memory: *"Police Seek Hit-and-Run Driver Who Killed 3-Year-Old Child."*

No.

I flip it over.

There's a handwritten message scrawled on the back. It says, *"You know who did this? I do. How would you like everyone else to know too, right before the election?"*

No, no, no.

Someone wants to destroy me.

My heart pounds in my chest.

But I won't be outmaneuvered so easily.

Adrenaline surges through my veins.

This means war.

I'd better form some alliances.

Not wanting to waste another second, I buzz Iris, my personal assistant, on my desk phone. She picks up on the first ring. "Yes, Mr. Cox?" Polite, efficient, smart. Thank God I gave her a good raise when we started this campaign. She's going to need to add discreet to that list of adjectives.

"Iris, may I speak to you in my office, please."

"Right away, sir."

Almost before the phone is back in its cradle, she's in the office, door closed, sitting in the chair opposite me, notebook in hand. I stuff the paper in the top drawer of my desk so she doesn't see it.

"Iris, an urgent matter has come up. I need it dealt with swiftly and confidentially. Whatever else you have on your plate can be delegated for the moment."

She nods.

"What security cameras do we have here at the office?" I ask. If there's video of the culprit tucking the envelope under the doormat, I have to see it.

"There are cameras covering every inch of the interior of the building, sir."

"And outside?"

"I'm not sure about the outside," she says. "I'll check on that for you right away." She jots herself a note.

"Please do," I say. "But first, I need you to get a hold of my father. He's in D.C., so he may be hard to track down, but this is an absolute emergency."

"Sir, is everything okay?" She seems genuinely concerned. Nice girl.

"Not exactly. I can't explain, but I need to speak to my father urgently."

"Yes, sir," she says.

"Also, please double-check the files to make sure we have a valid, signed, non-disclosure agreement from Kellen."

She stands up as she asks, "Is there anything else?"

"Not now, but if something does come up, it will be top priority. And please keep this completely confidential."

"Of course." She promises to update me as quickly as possible, and returns to her own desk.

I retrieve the note from the drawer to read it again. *"You know who did this? I do..."*

Who could have found out about the accident? It's my most closely guarded secret.

"How would you like everyone else to know too..."

It's going to get out. The whole story, including the accident and the subsequent cover-up. Someone's going to leak it to the press, if they haven't already.

I'll be ruined.

My chest tightens and my breathing gets shallow. Oh, God. Panic setting in.

Think. Who did this? Think.

Only three people in this world have ever known what happened that day.

Of course it's not my father. He would never try to sabotage me. He's the one who helped me cover it up in the first place.

His assistant Mary has been a trustworthy employee for three decades and my father compensates her very well. She doesn't have any motivation to betray our family.

Which leaves Cleo.

Yesterday I told her never to call me again. I rejected her, and now she's retaliating. It has to be her.

That venomous little traitor.

How can I make my appearances today? There are at least two campaign stops on the schedule, but all I want to do is jump in my car and go find Cleo, so I can throttle her until she swears not to sabotage my career.

I can't do this alone.

I grab the phone and buzz, wiping the sweat off my forehead. "Iris, I need my father."

"I'm working on that, sir. I'll connect you as soon as I reach him."

I slam the phone down harder than I mean to and cradle my head in my hands, trying desperately to get control of my racing mind.

26

Cleo

This morning I woke up a new woman, giddy with an unexpected sense of freedom. I'm determined not to need Mr. Cox any longer. He can go to Hell as far as I'm concerned. Or Washington, D.C. anyway. Same thing.

To celebrate my liberation from unrequited love, I've spent the morning in downtown Seattle. Coffee at my favorite shop, then grading midterms here in the magnificent glass atrium of the Central Library. I've just packed up my papers since I have to be back on campus in an hour.

As I'm taking a few more minutes to relax and watch the raindrops chase each other down the glass walls, my phone rings from inside my bag. I forgot to silence it.

It's him.

I wish I didn't care.

But I do. I can't ignore him.

Tossing my bag over my shoulder, I answer the phone.

"So I can't call you, but you can call me. Are those the rules?" I say, rushing past the glares of the other library patrons to the escalator.

"Cleo, are you trying to destroy me?"

"Excuse me?" I say. "You've demonstrated very clearly that I have no power over you."

"Don't you realize if you do this, you'll destroy yourself as well? Are you willing to lose your own career just to get back at me for rejecting you?"

I laugh, louder than I mean to. "Rejecting me? Please, Harris, obviously you weren't serious yesterday." I'm lying. He was dead serious and I know it.

Once at the bottom of the escalator, I stride through the concrete and glass of the first floor, then outside and around the corner to the first dry spot I see.

"You'll regret this, Cleo. I won't let you get away with it."

"Suppose you tone down the threats, Mr. Cox, and tell me precisely what you're accusing me of."

"Cleo, I got the envelope you left for me at the office," he says in a measured tone. He's obviously suppressing his anger. "I don't know what you're planning to do, but you've got to stop. You'll ruin us both."

"Harris," I say. "I never left you any envelope. You've got the wrong person."

A long silence passes. I think he's deciding whether he can trust me. He should.

Finally, he speaks. Quietly, so I have to strain to hear above the sound of traffic. "Someone left an envelope by the back door, with an anonymous note inside..." He trails off.

My heart beats faster. "What did it say?"

Even quieter now. "There's also a copy of the Seattle Times article, Cleo. About the accident."

Suddenly I feel exposed, vulnerable. I'm seized by a

throb of regret. Why did I answer this call? I shouldn't be talking to Harris. I've gotten caught in his web of deceit before and I don't want to be there again.

His voice breaks in on my private thoughts. "Are you listening to me? Someone sent me the *article*, Cleo."

A slow, creeping satisfaction spreads through my body. I'm reveling in his distress. Sometimes I surprise even myself.

"You've been caught," I say. "What are you going to do? Call your daddy?"

"My father, his assistant, and *you*," he spits, "are the only ones who know about this."

"You think I did this?" I say, indulging my self-righteous anger. "How dare you accuse me. I've been nothing but loyal to you since the day we met. If anything, it's you who's ruined *my* life—"

"Cleo, Cleo. Stop. I'm not accusing you," he says.

"You're the one who was driving that day, don't forget."

"I know. I'm sorry," he says. He speaks patiently, as if to a child. "Is there any chance you could have told someone else about this? At any time? It doesn't have to be recent. I just need to find—"

"Ryan." It's out of my mouth before I can think.

"Who?" he says.

"Ryan. I told you about him. My ex."

"Is this the guy who was your student?"

All at once, an idea blossoms into my mind, fully mature and ripe for the plucking. "Oh, Harris, it's been so awful," I say. "Ever since that night we had dinner together in your kitchen..."

"What does that have to do with this?" He sounds impatient.

"Never mind," I sigh. "I'm sorry to bother you. Forget I mentioned it."

"Cleo, please. Is this related to the matter at hand?"

"Well, it might be..."

"Out with it, Cleo," he says.

There's my invitation.

"Ryan's possessive. He frightens me. When we were together, he wanted to know where I was all the time. But when you and I started seeing each other a couple of weeks ago, I hid it from him because I wanted to protect you. Protect your campaign, your privacy. I assumed you wouldn't want any media attention on our relationship."

"We don't have a relationship," he says. He just can't stop digging his own hole.

Ignoring him, I go on. "He didn't like me spending time away from him, so one time he followed me. It was the night I went to your house and brought you dinner. He waited outside the entire time I was there, then followed me home afterward. He confronted me in the parking garage and forced me to admit who I was with."

"What exactly did you say?"

"I tried to say you were just an old friend, but he was grabbing my arm and wouldn't let go until—" I've never mastered tears on command, but I'm attempting to sound distraught. "Oh, Harris, I'm so sorry. He was going to hurt me. I had to tell him your name."

His voice low and controlled, Harris asks, "What else did you tell him?"

"Nothing! Nothing, I swear. But ever since, he's been so jealous. He's become obsessed with you, with finding out everything about you. You shouldn't underestimate him, he's scary. He's smart, too. Who knows what he could be planning?"

"Did he hurt you?" he asks.

"No. I only hope he doesn't hurt you," I say.

Through the phone, I hear a knocking, followed by a faint female voice in the background.

"I've got to go, Cleo. I have an important phone call coming in," he says.

"Of course," I say. I hope I've made an impression with my story.

"I need to locate this Ryan," he says.

"Yes, please do. For both of us."

"Cleo, I'm out of time. Just tell me where to find him, please."

I give him Ryan's full name and phone number.

"Is there anything else you need from me?" I ask. "I'm here to help, Harris."

Softly, he answers, "No, you've done more than enough. Thank you." Years of unspoken words fill the silence between us. Eventually, he adds, "You've been a good friend." And we both hang up.

I think I'll call this conversation a roaring success.

27

Harris

"Son. You've managed to pull me out of the dullest committee meeting on the Hill this morning. Should I be grateful or worried?"

The sound of my father's deep, authoritative voice tamps down my fear. No matter how anxious I become, he never fails to retain complete control.

"Dad, I've got a threat. I need your help to prevent a devastating leak to the press."

"All right, that sounds like something we can handle. Tell me everything you know. What is the information and who is threatening to leak it?"

Rubbing the tension out of my forehead with my free hand, I tell him about the envelope and its contents. He lays the blame on Cleo immediately.

"Damn that girl," he says. "We should have dealt with her more permanently back in 2003."

An unexpected stab of protectiveness pierces me.

"It wasn't her, Dad," I say. "I called her on the carpet this morning and she insisted she didn't do it."

"And you believe her?"

"Yes, I do," I say. "She did give me a lead on who might have, though. An ex-boyfriend of hers."

"So she didn't keep her mouth shut. This is what I was afraid of," he says. "We're going to need a strategy to handle her."

"I'm telling you, Dad, I don't think it was her. She's kept this secret for fifteen years. Why would she leak it now?"

"I don't know, son, that's a good question," he says. "Has she been provoked in some way? What kind of contact have you had with her?"

This conversation is headed in the wrong direction. Nothing good can come from my father knowing about me seeing Cleo.

"Dad, I think you ought to start with her ex-boyfriend, as I mentioned." I give him a quick summary of everything Cleo told me about Ryan's jealousy and obsessive behavior.

"If this really is nothing more than a simple matter of a disgruntled lover, he shouldn't give us too much trouble," he says. "Do you have a name or any contact information for this young man?"

I provide him Ryan's name and phone number.

"We'll definitely check into him. But I'm most concerned with Ms. Tait," he says.

He's not going to let this go. "Dad, I—"

"Son, you called for my help. Now you let me do what needs to be done."

Have I made a mistake involving my father and his people? What if I've put Cleo in danger?

"So what now?" I ask, swallowing down my objections.

"Our highest priority is to keep the incriminating information from getting out." His tone is deliberate. "At all costs. Do you understand what I'm saying?"

I don't like where this is going, but it's out of my hands now. My father wouldn't fail to protect my career even if I asked him to.

"Yes," I say.

A wild thought bursts into my head. *I still love this volatile woman.* But my career can't survive if our relationship does, so I bury the thought.

"We'll put together a plan to deal with her and her boyfriend," my father says.

"Ex-boyfriend," I say.

"Number one, we need details on this girl. How much do you know about her current life?"

Massaging my temples, I try to push away the feeling that I've made a disastrous mistake. My father has received my distress signal and converted it into a full-blown seek-and-destroy mission. Even though I can't stop the inevitable, I'm not sure I want to conspire any deeper.

"I don't know too much about her," I lie.

"That's all right. I didn't expect you to. I've got some resources I can allocate to this immediately. We'll pull a background check, find out where she works, whether she has any family we can exploit."

The back of my throat convulses. What have I done?

"Is that necessary?" I ask.

He chuckles in a way that nauseates me. "We'll pursue every avenue available to us, including using family as leverage."

Thalia is going to get dragged into this. No.

"Stick to your campaign schedule today, son. Don't cancel any appearances. Get out there and win those votes."

"Yes, Dad," I choke.

28

Cleo

I'm working late into the night in my office, grading term papers. Not because I want to, but because today has been so bizarre I can't bear the thought of going home to my condo alone. If I sit there in the quiet, I will go crazy thinking about Harris. All the things he's done to me and all the things I've done to him. So I distract myself with a stack of freshman psych papers.

A panicky knocking on my door breaks my concentration. It sounds urgent. Who could be looking for me at this hour of the night?

I wait for them to go away, but the pounding only becomes more insistent. Whoever's there isn't leaving. I decide that if I'm going to answer, I can't be timid.

Lunging for the handle, I yank the door open. As soon as I do, I see Ryan standing there, red-faced.

I do not want to talk to him.

"Office hours are in the morning, Ryan. You can come back tomorrow." I move to close the door, but he sticks his foot out to prevent it from latching.

"I can't come back later. This is an emergency." He pushes past in such a frenzy, he almost knocks me backward. His aggressiveness puts me on edge. He seems out of control, and I'm afraid of what he might do.

"Sit down, please," he says. I obey.

He runs both hands through his hair and paces the room in a circle.

Hoping to avoid inflaming his temper any further, I decide to affect a professional demeanor with him.

"Ryan, you seem upset. Why don't we call a counselor in here? I'm not the right person to talk you through whatever you're dealing with. After all, we did agree to end our non-professional relationship." I reach for the office phone.

"No. No, just talk to me for a minute. Please."

"Then you'll need to be specific about what's happening."

"Someone is watching me. Or spying. I keep getting these weird phone calls all day. And there's a black SUV that's been parked outside my apartment for hours. When I tried to leave, it followed me here—"

"Why would a black SUV be following you?"

Ryan sighs. "It started this morning with the phone calls. I was at the Halloween store, shopping for a costume to go out with friends this weekend. I thought I might try to meet a new girl, since you—"

"Stay on track for me, Ryan. What phone calls?" I ask.

"I didn't recognize the number, so at first I didn't answer. But the person kept calling again and again and again. So finally I answered just to get rid of them."

"Who was it?"

"A man's voice, threatening. He said if I released 'the information' to the media I would be targeted and destroyed or some weird thing like that. I thought it was a stupid Halloween prank, so I forgot about it."

"That's what it was, a prank." Of course, I know better.

"But then this afternoon after I got back home, they called again. The same guy's voice told me I had to hand over any proof I had or they would destroy my future, get me kicked out of school."

"Proof of what?" I ask.

"I have no idea," he says, grabbing his hair in his fists. "That's when I noticed the dude in the black SUV sitting outside watching me. For a whole hour he sat in front of my apartment until he got sick of waiting for me, I guess. He came to the door and pounded on it until I had no choice but to answer. He was serious. Like deadly serious. He had a gun. He told me he was there to pick up any documents that I had pertaining to that guy running for Congress, Harris Cox."

"Mr. Cox?" I say. "Do you even know him?"

"I've seen signs around for his campaign, but I don't pay attention to that stuff. I swore to the dude with the gun that I didn't have any documents. He didn't believe me. He even asked if he could come in and search my place. When I told him no, he stood there for a minute, like he was deciding what to do. I swear he was going to come in and do it, anyway. But his phone rang, and whoever called must have changed his mind because he left."

"I'm at a loss as to why you're here, Ryan. How does this relate to me?" Damn, I'm good at this. Professional, impartial, and convincing. Keeping all these lies straight is an advanced skill.

"I need your help. These guys are scaring me, and I want you to talk to Cox. Tell him to call off his dogs."

"This is absurd, Ryan. I don't have any contact with Harris Cox."

"Come on, Cleo, don't lie to me."

"What?"

"About a month ago, we were in here, doing what we do... And you told me this story about how you and him used to go to college together, here in the Psych department."

I sigh. He's right, I did tell that story. I'd forgotten about it, but now that he mentions it... I was feeling angry one day, brooding about how if Harris hadn't left me I'd have a life with him instead of enacting clandestine affairs with students in my office. Ryan never mentioned it again, so I assumed he'd forgotten. Obviously not.

One little mistake isn't the end of the world. I can fix this.

"You're right," I say. "I did say I was acquainted with Harris in the past. But that doesn't mean I have access to him now. He's an important man. Sorry, I can't help you."

Ryan stares at me for a long, uncomfortable moment. To break the tension, I pick up a pen and shuffle some papers, trying to send the message that I'm getting back to work. Clearly, Ryan is not ready for the conversation to be over. Instead of leaving, he paces back and forth, ratcheting up the tension in the room. For a fleeting moment, I think he's going to leave until he roars and punches the stuffed leather chair. It's loud. And violent. I'm afraid of what else he might do.

I seize the phone to alert campus security, but he lurches forward, forcing my hand down to prevent me from calling out.

"All right, I'm sorry I overreacted, okay? I need your help," he says.

I don't say a word, just look at him and wait for him to continue. He's unstable and I don't want to agitate him.

"Cleo, please." He advances toward me. I back into the

corner as he comes around the desk, invading my personal space. He grabs both my wrists, hard, and I flinch with pain. He's strong. I try to wrestle free, but I can't. "I need you to get in touch with Cox's people, or whoever. Just tell them it wasn't me. I don't have any information."

"I don't know that you don't have anything," I say, wrenching my wrists as forcefully as I can. Still, they don't budge out of his grip. He squeezes tighter.

"I don't. It's not me. You know it's not me. Tell them."

"Or what?" I ask. His aggression scares me, but I'll be damned if I'm going to let this nerdy little paramour force me to do anything I don't want to do.

His eyes are savage, like a trapped wild beast. "Whoever is threatening to release this stuff, if they do release it, these guys will suspect it was me. And they'll retaliate, or punish me, or whatever. Maybe even kill me. They have guns."

"Fine. I'll call his office. But I won't promise you anything." His arms go slack and he releases my wrists with a deep exhale.

"Thank you. That's all I... thank you," he says.

"Now get out of here."

He slinks out without another word.

5 Days Before Election Day

29

Cleo

The usual damp chill of the autumn air cuts through me as Thalia and I meander the walking paths, dodging the occasional oblivious kite-flier. We met for a stroll today at Gas Works Park, the most ironic place in Seattle. The ruins of the old coal gasification plant stand watch over the rolling green hill that conceals a mountain of industrial sludge. Couples loll on the grass, soaking up whatever meager sun they can get in the Northwest. Children play on the remains of the filthy, polluting factory equipment made palatable by their bright, colorful paint jobs.

A toxic waste dump covered by a thin veneer of civility, and people love it.

Pulling my new red trench coat tighter around me, I suppress a yawn. I'm regretting the decision to come here. I'm cold, I'm tired, and my feet hurt from walking in these heels. A nice, toasty coffee shop would solve all those problems right now.

That confrontation with Ryan yesterday overstimulated me and I wasn't able to get any sleep last night. After I finally got him out of my office, I was wired. The way I'd kept my composure in the face of his aggressive tantrum, the way I'd manipulated him into believing everything I said... I was crackling with pride. For once, I was the one in control, and it felt exhilarating.

Since there was no way I was going to focus on work after that, I went home.

But before I even got to my car, I was thinking of Harris again. Reliving the events of the last two days evaporated every drop of that delicious self-satisfaction.

I couldn't lie to myself that I was in control. Not after what I saw.

The image of Harris's silhouette at the window, kissing that other woman, haunted me all night long. Even when I drifted off to sleep, the two of them popped up in my dreams. A mix of jealousy and anxiety has gripped me since I gave up and got out of bed this morning.

Spending time with Thalia was my attempt to defuse my agitation. I've contemplated telling her what I'm going through with Harris. Of course I can't reveal the accident, but I can talk to her about our relationship issues. Maybe she'll reassure me that everything will work out, that Harris and I will finally be together permanently.

So far, though, she's spent the whole time chattering about her problems with Warren and the girls.

I tune her out for a few minutes, taking in the view of the Seattle skyline across Lake Union. I'm trying to figure out how to broach the subject of Harris. How much can I tell her? Can I give her some idea of what's going on without divulging too much?

Just when I'm ready to dive in, she beats me to it.

"Cleo, I have something to tell you." I'm both frustrated and relieved. "Can you keep a secret?"

Little does she know I've been keeping a monumental

one for fifteen years. "Of course," I say.

She takes a deep breath, bites her lip for a minute, then says, "I've met someone."

The magnitude of this confession has me speechless. Thalia is a good girl. I've always been the naughty one.

"A man?" I say stupidly.

She gives the tiniest nod. "I think I'm in love."

She wants my approval.

"I have to ask, what about Warren?" I don't have any affection for Warren, but there are consequences to cheating in a marriage.

"Please don't do that," she says. "Don't bring Warren into it."

"I think he's already in, don't you?"

"This isn't about Warren, it's about me! I've found someone who treats me like a queen, and I love it. I love *him*." She's clearly smitten and feeling defiant about it.

"Are you seeing this man? Dating? Or just... fantasizing?" How deep a hole has she dug for herself?

Her phone rings just in time to save her from having to respond. She peeks at it and blushes a deep pink. "This will only take a second," she says. She turns away from me to answer. The conversation is brief, and she talks in a whisper so I can't hear what she says, but after the call she's lit up and her eyes are sparkling.

"Speak of the devil," I say.

"Don't look at me like that, Cleo." My disapproval must be showing. "You have a new boyfriend every week."

"Yes, well, I'm not married," I say.

"It's my turn now to have some fun," she says. "I should never have settled down with Warren so early."

"So, who's the lucky guy?" I ask, suppressing an eye roll. She's acting foolish and immature, but I won't hold her to some standard of moral purity I can't uphold myself. I do want her to be happy.

"I'm not telling yet," she says. Her eyes twinkle with mischief. "But I'm sure you'll love him."

"As long as you know what you're doing," I say. "You could get into a heap of trouble dating someone while you're still married to Warren. Are you sure this is what you want?"

"Right now, yes."

"And you've considered how this will affect the girls?" I'm not a parent, but I'm pretty sure they're supposed to consider things like that.

"They don't have to know," she says.

It's clear she hasn't thought this all the way through, but it's none of my business. She's a grown adult. "Then I'll leave you to it. Enjoy yourself," I say.

We finish our trek around the loop trail and I suggest we go to a coffee shop. Maybe I can talk to her there, next to a fireplace with a hot drink in my hand. I'm still drowning in anxiety over the state of my relationship with Harris, and I'm hoping she'll lend me some of her optimism.

But today is not my lucky day.

"Sorry, I can't," she says. "My man needs me."

"Seriously?"

She bites her lip and nods her head. "I have to duck in and visit before the girls get home from school. Sorry."

"Good to see you're already choosing him over your own sister." I sound resentful because I am.

Thalia doesn't take it to heart. She swats at my shoulder. "Oh, don't be like that, Cleo. Be happy for me."

"Sure," I say, wondering when was the last time I was happy for anyone.

30

Thalia

I wasn't honest with Cleo, which bothers me. Since I was a kid, I've always been honest with her. She insisted upon it. If I neglected to finish my homework or forgot to do some of my chores, she sat me down and made me confess. She didn't have to push me too hard, because I seem to have been born with an unfortunate flaw. The desperate need to do what's right.

But lately I've been questioning that. Who determines what's right? Common sense? Conventional wisdom? Tradition? Law? Every single one of those is a negotiable concept.

So I've been pondering the idea that maybe doing what's right simply means... doing what's right for me. It's time I put myself first, something I've never done in all my life.

Still, fudging the truth to Cleo doesn't sit well. Even though it wasn't an outright lie, it's a stretch. I'll have to get over that.

My man doesn't need me, at least not right this minute.

I just wanted to get away. Something about Cleo lately niggles at me. Her energy feels desperate, clingy. All I want is to enjoy the exhilarating freedom I've found, and her presence drags me down.

As Cleo and Gas Works Park disappear into my rearview mirror, I find myself smiling like a lunatic. James's photo gallery is still a good half hour drive away, but I can't wait to get there. I crank up the music in my car and sing loud and off-key the whole way there.

When I arrive, my heart flutters. I've never done this before.

I take a deep breath, tug down my jacket, and tiptoe inside. A little bell tinkles, and I survey the gallery as I wait for James to appear. The walls are covered with photographs of the cities of the world. Some of them are large enough to cover half the wall in my living room. All of a sudden, I wish I was more cultured. I've never studied art, nor even really looked at it. I have no idea what to think.

Which cities are featured in the photos? I don't know. Are the close-ups or the skylines better? I don't know. Is black and white more sophisticated than color? I don't know that either.

Just when I'm feeling overwhelmed with my own ignorance, James emerges from the back of the gallery. He takes my hand gently and kisses it. "Mademoiselle," he says, as a lock of hair falls over his eye. "Welcome to my home away from home. You look positively fetching."

I blush, just the way I did when I first met him in the coffee shop with Cleo and Amber.

He's not French, but he acts exactly the way I imagine a sexy young French artist would act. I guess his time in Paris taught him well. He's irresistible.

"Allow me to show you the prints I've curated for you,"

he says. He leads me into a back room in the gallery, placing a hand on my lower back. My pulse accelerates as I remember what I'm here for.

All the photos he's laid out for me are of Seattle, as I had requested when we talked on the phone. He's chosen a varied assortment of scenes: the Space Needle at sunset, Pike Place Market bustling with people, Mount Rainier through the mist, and the city skyline at night. But one stands out to me above all the others.

I point to the small photo of an empty bench on a beach facing the Puget Sound, raging with whitewater on a windy day.

"This is the one," I say. "I like it. I don't know why." I feel like I should apologize. He has all these grand, gorgeous prints to choose from, and I pick the tiny, abandoned bench. It *is* just right, but like I told James, I don't know why.

"No matter, chérie. When we know, we know."

I pay for the print, he wraps it up, and we exchange goodbyes, complete with another kiss on the hand.

James certainly knows how to treat a lady. He makes it look so easy. Why does it seem so impossible for Warren?

31

Harris

Today has held a full schedule of campaign appearances, which is keeping me busy enough to avoid brooding about my father's plans. This afternoon we're at the University of Washington, which has me thinking of Cleo. She's texted me more than once since we spoke yesterday, wanting to check up on me. Normal behavior for her, so I trust she isn't in any danger at the moment.

Regardless, I've been plagued by nerves, knowing that she works on campus. I haven't told her about my appearance here; I hope she doesn't find out and show up to make a scene.

As I'm shaking hands dutifully with a group of politically active students, Iris comes up behind me and whispers in my ear. "Sir, your father's on the line."

I excuse myself and take the phone she presses into my hand. When I look down, I'm startled to see my fingers trembling. The sight of this weakness floods me with bitterness. I'll be damned if I let this situation make a coward out of me.

Full of resolve, I answer. "Dad. What have we got?"

"Good news, son. We have a solid action plan to suppress this leak before it ever sees the light of day. As far as we can determine through our contacts now, no news outlets are aware of any negative items about you. Are you free to discuss specifics about where we go from here?"

"Not exactly. I'm finishing up an appearance right now, and then we've got another stop after this. What can you tell me briefly?"

"First, the boyfriend angle turned out to be a dead end. He's been investigated thoroughly and we're pretty sure he's not the culprit."

"So it's not Ryan?" I say. "You're sure?"

"He's still on the radar, but not the prime suspect."

"So now what?" I ask.

"As was my first instinct, we've got to look closely at Ms. Tait. I've got some people digging up the necessary information right now. As soon as they have what we need, we'll get her neutralized."

"Dad," I hiss under my breath. "I do not want anyone hurt." It's out of my mouth before I even realize what I'm saying.

"No, no, that shouldn't be necessary. But we will do whatever it takes to make sure that this girl is contained."

"She's not a *girl*, Dad, she's a woman." The sharpness of my tone surprises even me. I must get my feelings under control.

"Son, is there some element of relationship between you and Ms. Tait that I need to know about?"

"No," I lie. "Absolutely not."

"Good. Now, the second part of the plan involves me flying out to Seattle to make a campaign appearance with you. Mary's had a devil of a time clearing my schedule to come out there, but this is important. The good press will make a nice bump for you right before the election."

"All right, just have Mary give Iris a call when you've finalized your travel plans. I've got to hang up now, Dad, unless there's anything else pressing you need to tell me."

"Yes, there is," he says. I signal to Iris that I can't get off the phone quite yet. She announces that the meeting is ended, and the students file out of the room.

"I need you to focus on this for me, son. This part of the plan I need you to carry out. It involves Ms. Tait's younger sister, a Mrs. Thalia Edwards."

No, no, no. This is exactly what I wanted to avoid. What the hell does he expect me to do?

"No, Dad. No family members. Just find Cleo and keep her quiet. That shouldn't be too hard. We're not bringing innocent people into this."

"Listen to me, son." It's a command, not a request. "What I'm about to suggest is not optional. This Cleo of yours is unpredictable. She's a danger to your future. If she were so easy to keep quiet, we wouldn't be taking these emergency measures days before your first election. This is not just your political future at stake, it's mine." He pauses for dramatic effect, the force of his will filling the silence.

"One thing I have never done," he says, "is to do anything halfway. So here is what I need from you."

He orders me to contact Thalia, instructing me what to say. He dictates her phone number, which I don't bother to write down.

I'm uneasy about this, but he has a point. My political future is at stake, and I can't let a fifteen-year-old mistake destroy it all.

32

Cleo

Was I wrong about Amber?

I've been pondering this question since Thalia zoomed out of the Gas Works parking lot this morning. I was certain Amber was the woman Harris was seeing. The one he kissed in his living room.

But something vexes me. When I showed Harris the photo of her and Ryan, he didn't flinch. In fact, he didn't even look closer at the photo.

If I were in his shoes… If someone showed me a picture of Harris kissing a different woman, you can be damn sure I would take a closer look. I would want to know exactly who the tramp was and whether or not Harris was enjoying it.

Harris has been known to be a good liar, of course, but that doesn't explain away his behavior. The only rationalization for his total nonchalance is that he actually doesn't care who Amber is kissing.

Which means that he doesn't care about Amber.

This is not good news. It means the elaborate plan I

staged at the Wellness Center was pointless. Worse, it means I have no idea who I'm competing against for Harris's affections.

I can't eliminate her unless I know who she is.

There has to be a way to find out.

33

Thalia

I thought I understood men. Dating Warren was easy and straightforward. He asked me out on a date, we hit it off, and then I became his girlfriend. After a while, things got serious and I married him.

But this time around, things are much more opaque. I'd say that we've been seeing each other for a few weeks now, but that seems entirely the wrong name for it. We've only been alone together once during that time. Almost our entire relationship has been conducted on the phone, both talking and texting.

I've tried to use my feminine wiles to hint at my desire to be with him, to no avail. He avoids discussing it, putting it off until some future point in time. And yet he's incredibly affectionate and sweet on the phone. Is this normal now? Does everybody just talk and text instead of seeing each other? The way I remember it, when you're in love with someone, you can't tear yourself away from them.

Maybe I've been married so long I forgot how to date.

Nevertheless, I can't wait for his phone call tonight. During the day, it's almost impossible to find much time to talk because he's always surrounded by people and I have to find time away from my family. Instead, he's made a ritual of calling me during this little window of time, after the girls are in bed but before Warren gets home. It's become my favorite part of the day. I live for it.

While I wait, I take the photo of the empty bench out of its brown paper wrapping. Why did I choose this one? That sad, forlorn bench is crying to be filled with a loving, snuggling couple. Maybe I wish it could be me. Gazing out at the wind and the waves huddling with him under his jacket.

I wonder if we'll ever get that chance. With Warren tying me down, and with his career governing his life, it might be too much to ask. But I close my eyes and dream for just a moment until my phone interrupts my reverie.

It's him.

The man I've always dreamed of.

The man who's sweeping me off my feet.

Harris Cox.

4 Days Before Election Day

34

Thalia

"Daisy! Dot! Breakfast is ready!"

After spending a full forty-five minutes getting ready this morning, we've got to hurry. I went through four different outfits before settling on navy dress pants, a white blouse, and gold jewelry. Professional, but not too flashy. I even styled my hair and put on make-up. We're running late now, but today is far too important for my usual yoga pants and ponytail routine.

The girls come squealing into the kitchen just as I'm pouring milk in their cereal. I'm about to switch the television channel from the morning news over to cartoons when the story catches my attention.

"With just days to go, the race for the U.S. Congressional seat for the 7th District is heating up," says the anchor. "Polls show candidate Harris Cox's slim lead over opponent Tim Johnson has now evaporated in the wake of a lackluster debate performance Tuesday night. Cox, the son of U.S. Senator William Cox, was the favorite to win until he suffered a medical collapse at a rally weeks ago. Johnson now leads by two percentage points, which is within the margin of error."

Onto the screen strides Harris, in a clip from a recent campaign appearance. Shaking hands, brandishing that disarming smile. Making profound connections with those deep, soulful, brown eyes.

My hand flies to my breast, trying to calm the fluttering of my heart. I can't wait to see him today. I'm so excited that for a minute, I even forget my husband is sleeping in the next room.

"Mommy! Turn on our show!" Daisy's loud whine breaks in on my fantasy.

"Sorry, Daise, here you go." I switch the cartoons on, grab my phone off the counter, and head into the living room. "Eat quick, it's time to go," I call to the girls, who are already giggling so loud it hurts my ears.

Searching the internet I find the story on all the local news sites. It's true, Harris is behind in the polls now. It seems impossible he could lose the election, though. Why would anyone not vote for him? He's so charismatic and charming. And smart.

The clock on my phone tells me we have to leave or we're going to be late for school.

And my first day of work.

Last night I was so eager to talk on the phone with Harris. Just hearing his deep voice warms me like the heat of a fire on a misty, cold night. But the conversation was less than satisfying. In fact, it would be accurate to say it was a little awkward. He seemed different, kind of formal. I told myself he was just tired from campaigning all day, but I'm worried about him. Maybe the stress is getting overwhelming.

But I'll be able to check on him soon, if we can ever get out of the house.

The girls' uncontrollable giggling is driving me crazy. "Enough!" I yell. "Get your backpacks and get in the car. Now. School time."

I'm nervous. In less than half an hour I'll be starting a job, temporary though it may be. I don't know the first thing about working on a political campaign. But Harris needs help. He insisted I work for him as his personal assistant, at least for the next few days leading up to the election. I protested that he should get someone more experienced, since it's been years since I had a job.

"It has to be you, Thalia," he said. "It has to."

How could I say no to that?

As the girls load themselves noisily into the car, I consider waking Warren to say goodbye since I won't be home until the afternoon. I walk into the bedroom and realize the foolishness of that idea. I could shake him awake but he'll just roll over, give me a groggy "hmmm?" and fall right back to sleep, snoring, before I can even leave the room.

Leaving him to his beauty sleep, I join the girls in the car. Their school is only eight minutes away, and we somehow make it on time. "Hey, you little monsters," I say. "Give Mommy a hug before you go inside. See you after school."

I drive on to the campaign office, cold sweat threatening to ruin my freshly ironed white blouse. When I arrive, I go in through the front door and just sort of hover. The office is fairly small. There aren't that many employees, but they all look busy and important. I'm not sure who to talk to. Fortunately, a young man at a nearby desk takes pity on me. "Can I help you?" he asks.

"I'm Harris's — um, *Mr. Cox's* new assistant," I say.

He looks surprised, or maybe nervous. "New assistant — Okay, I don't — Umm — Let me check with Iris."

The timid young man leaves me hovering by the entrance again while he disappears into the bowels of the office. I feel like an impostor. I belong at home, washing the dishes in my yoga pants.

After a couple of minutes, he comes back. "Mr. Cox's office is in the back. Follow me."

My heart leaps in my chest, beating faster with each step.

He knocks before opening an unmarked door. Harris is sitting behind a desk. His private office is much more modest than I expected. "Thank you, Kellen," he says to the man. Kellen nods and closes the door behind him.

I'm alone in this little room with Harris.

If I was hoping for romance or a gesture of affection, I quickly realize I'm not going to get it. He's familiar, but perfunctory.

"Thank you for agreeing to this, Thalia. It's very important to me to have you here," he says.

"I don't exactly know what I'm doing here yet," I say. "That woman made it seem like you already have an assistant."

"Yes, I have Iris. But she handles more of my business affairs. You, on the other hand, will be here for more personal needs. Moral support." He flashes me that dazzling smile, though I notice his eyes look strained. "You'll accompany me to my campaign appearances today."

His desk phone buzzes. "Sir, I apologize for interrupting," says a female voice. "Your car is ready."

"Thank you, Iris. Please notify security that Mrs. Edwards will travel with me today," he says.

I don't know why Harris asked me to do this. I guess I'll figure it out as I go.

35

Harris

Thalia's been by my side all morning.

I hate it.

She's lovely. Helpful, friendly, sweet, attentive... and I've never felt more guilty.

There's not really anything for her to do on the campaign trail. All the necessary roles are filled, but she's enterprisingly created a job for herself. She's been tending to my clothes and hair, making sure I look as picture perfect as a good candidate should.

Her demeanor has been professional and restrained. Not a hint of impropriety could be detected between us.

She's an extraordinary woman. She deserves better than me. Better than her pathetic husband, too.

I can't handle this. I'm already collapsing under the weight of all this stress. Dealing with my conflicting feelings about Thalia might just break me.

Damn my father for bringing her into this mess. She doesn't know she's just being used.

36

Harris

The ache behind my left eye is back. I had a few blissful weeks without it, beginning the day Cleo waltzed into my hospital room. But now it's come back with a vengeance. The squeezing pressure is almost intolerable after that respite. But I'm functioning.

I could use Thalia's tender touch right now, but she already left to pick up her girls from school.

The campaign marches on.

I've just finished a successful afternoon with the firefighters at the Queen Anne fire station. We've gotten promises of votes and even picked up a handful of additional volunteers to help us knock on doors this last weekend before the election. I'm smiling through my misery, hoping it comes out looking like more than a grimace.

At the moment, I'm being treated to a series of stomach-churning paramedic horror stories by a jovial firefighter named Jerome, who must be at least six-foot-five and 350 pounds. I'm laughing as expected, but suppressing the urge to retch. Just as I can't take one more gory description of a broken, protruding bone, Iris swoops in to the rescue.

"I'm sorry to interrupt, gentlemen, but I'm going to steal the candidate for a moment."

Jerome claps me on the back with his massive hand, causing me to stumble forward as we walk away from the group.

"Thank you, Iris, I think I was about to lose my lunch," I say under my breath.

"I'm glad I could help. But I really do have important news for you," she says, as she leads me over to an empty corner of the firehouse. "I've just heard from your father's assistant, Mary. She gave me a message for you regarding your father's visit. He'll be flying in tomorrow night and will do a joint appearance with you on Sunday."

"Great. Go ahead and do whatever's necessary to rearrange the schedule," I say.

"One more thing," she says. "Your father wanted you notified he has initiated an investigation into your person of interest."

The pain in my eye throbs again until I feel like it's going to pop out. I press on it with my free hand. "Did he give a name?"

"I'm sorry. I don't have any further information on that."

It doesn't matter. I know he means Cleo.

I have a sudden compulsion to get out of here. I want to jump in that fire truck and order Jerome to speed over to Cleo's condo, or her office, or wherever she is right now. She needs my protection. So does Thalia. This whole thing has spiraled out of control. What are my father's people going to do to them? I don't want either of them hurt.

But I have an image to maintain and an election to win. There are too many people involved for me to blow my chance at winning a seat in Congress. Not to mention too much money. I'm obligated now, and I have to continue. Doing anything else would be political and career suicide.

Taking a deep breath, I give my shoulders a shake. I paste on my famous politician's grin and head back over to Jerome and his cohorts. "Well, guys, thank you for a great lunch. We're so grateful to you for all you do. You're the real deal. True heroes."

I shake everyone's hand and get a few aggressive buddy hugs from some more of the lighthearted men. We take a group photo, and I turn to give a last wave before heading out.

Sinking into the back seat of the car, I'm exhausted. More so than I should be.

Why did someone have to dredge up the past like this? Everything's been fine for fifteen years, but now someone is turning a tragic mistake into a threat. For what? To punish me?

My father will protect me, but either Cleo or Thalia will end up getting hurt, whether I want them to or not.

Maybe both of them.

The stress makes me feel like I might throw up. Those stories from Jerome didn't help.

Fury boils up from my gut like hot acid. Damn Cleo. It's her fault. If she didn't deliver that envelope to the office herself, she must have told someone who did.

She deserves whatever my father can dish out. I won't let her destroy me. It's as simple as that.

37

Cleo

He isn't here. At least I don't think he is.

The sheers are closed, but the drapes are open, as usual. I don't detect any movement in the front room, and his car isn't parked in the driveway.

On Fridays, I can get away with leaving work early, so I drove straight to Harris's house from my office. I've been stewing all day about him. He's not responding to my texts, and I can't stand not knowing any more.

Who is the other woman he was kissing Tuesday night?

I hated him so much when I saw them together. How could he do that to me, after everything we've been through together? But maybe I don't hate him. Maybe it's just love. Deep, intense, irreplaceable.

I don't know what I'm doing here. I didn't plan it out. Right now, I'm sitting in my car, staring at the front of his perfect house, reliving the horror of the moment I saw him kissing that other woman.

Impulsively, I jump out of my car and bound up the steps to the front door. I'll find out whether or not he's home. First, I knock on the door. No answer. I try ringing the bell. Still no answer. Now what?

I peek behind myself, glancing down the street on both sides. It's empty of cars, and no one is walking down the sidewalk. Okay. I creep around the side of the house. The garage is behind the house, so I just walk the driveway until I'm in the tiny backyard. I've never been back here. It's plain. The grass is neglected. There's no patio furniture or potted plants. Apparently Harris only prioritizes the areas of the home that people will see.

There is a back door to the house, though. From my memory of the inside, I figure this must lead into the kitchen. I don't remember seeing a door, so maybe there's a mud room. I walk up to look through the window. I turn the handle. You've got to be kidding.

It's unlocked.

Harris needs better security. With one more quick glance around the yard, I open the door and go in, grateful that Harris doesn't have a dog.

Clapping my hands over my mouth to suppress a cry, I can't believe I have free rein of Harris's house! I don't even know how this happened. I wasn't planning to break in, but here I am. So now what do I do? What do I want to know about Harris?

I already know everything I want to know about Harris.

It's *her* I know nothing about. Who is this evil tramp? Is she sleeping here? God, I hope not. But if so, maybe she's left some personal items. Toothbrush, perfume, nightgown... I'll see what I can find.

The kitchen is in perfect order. All dishes put away, counters clear, floor clean. Like a crime scene after it's been scrubbed. I won't find any trace of her in this room.

The bedroom. I didn't see Harris's bedroom the only

other time I was here. My breath catches in my throat as I approach the door at the end of the short hall. This has to be it. The door is ajar, and I push it open. There is a huge king-size bed with a sleek headboard, all made up tidily with a down comforter in a gray duvet. This place is impossibly clean. Who does this? But I won't be dissuaded. There has to be some trace of her somewhere.

I remove the throw pillows, peel back the comforter and blanket. Nothing. I don't know what I expected, some black lace panties stuck in between the hospital corners of the sheets? I smooth the comforter back and try to replace the copious pillows as they were. Hopefully, I got that right.

Okay, onto the dresser. Nothing incriminating on any flat surfaces in here. The only thing on the dresser is an empty vase. There are two dressers in here, part of a matching set with the bed. The low, wide one has six drawers in it, and the tall, narrow one has five. I'll start with the low one, since it reminds me of a guest dresser in a hotel room. Maybe she'll keep some extra clothes in here.

My heart beats faster in anticipation of what I might find. I open the top left drawer, and find nothing in it but two remote controls. One for the flat screen TV mounted to the wall above the dresser, and one for the streaming device connected to it. Must be so Harris can keep up with the twenty-four hour news cycle.

Next is the top right drawer. Completely empty.

I open all the rest of the drawers in this dresser, and they're all empty. What an odd thing to discover. Where are all his clothes?

Next, I check the tall dresser. Not even anticipating what might be here, I'm stunned when I open the top drawer to find Harris's neatly folded underwear. I stop in my tracks. Losing any sense of propriety I may have once had, I lift out the pair on top. Sleek black boxer briefs. I almost smell them, but I refrain. I just hold them up, picture Harris in them, memorize the picture, then fold them perfectly and put them back. I'm careful, so he won't be able to tell they've been moved. I will see him in those some day. And out of them. Soon.

I scan the rest of the drawers in the dresser, finding nothing that could belong to a woman. Same thing in the closet. Just Harris's clean and pressed shirts and suits, and a collection of expensive shoes.

Then I see the bathroom door. Of course. But no luck. There's no toothbrush here, no hairbrush, no tampons under the sink. I don't know what I thought I would do with a toothbrush if I found it. It's not like I could have it analyzed for DNA.

Just as I'm about to give up, I notice the laundry hamper. Lifting the lid, I find dirty clothes. Actual dirty clothes. The only thing in the entire house that isn't cleaned, polished, and sanitized. I rummage through the hamper, relishing the faint smell of Harris's sweat. One pair of pajamas, one dress shirt, one undershirt, a pair of socks, and a pair of black boxer briefs. And only one bath towel. Whoever she is, she must not be spending the night. There's no trace of her.

Noticing the clock on the bathroom wall, I realize it's almost five o'clock. Harris probably won't be back for hours, but other people in the neighborhood will be coming home from work soon. I don't want anyone to see me and know I was here. Time to split.

I take a quick glance at the guest bathroom in the hallway. Nothing there either. I didn't inspect the living room other than a cursory glance around the immaculate space, but if there's no sign of her in the master bedroom or bath, there won't be anything here either.

Is she even real? I'm questioning myself now. Maybe I imagined Harris kissing her. It was my worst fear, and I'd drunk too much wine, and I just dreamed the whole thing. I'm feeling unsettled now. But it's time to go before I get caught.

Pausing just long enough in the kitchen to remember the evening we spent here a few weeks ago, I go out the back door, leaving it unlocked, just the way I found it.

I also made sure to turn off all the lights and put everything back exactly the way it was, including the underwear. He'll never know I was here.

Unfortunately, I'm no closer to finding out who he's cheating on me with.

38

Thalia

"Thank you so much, Emily. I should be home no later than ten o'clock." Warren would think I splurged on a babysitter tonight, if he even knew I was out. But I don't have to justify myself to him, since my sister is the one who just saved our house. The girls are already in bed, and I've cleaned the dinner dishes and thrown another load of laundry in the machine. "Text me if there's an emergency."

As I'm about to leave, an idea strikes me.

"Oops, I forgot something," I say to Emily. I hurry to the fridge, not wanting to waste a moment, and pack up a couple of the brownies I made yesterday, before I was a working woman. "Thanks, I'll text you when I'm on the way home," I call on my way out.

In the car, I position the brownies carefully on the passenger seat, next to my handbag, which conceals the gift-wrapped photo I bought from James. Then I call Warren before driving off. We don't have a new enough vehicle to have a BlueTooth, so I can't talk while driving.

"Hey, babe," he yells over the din in the restaurant. "What's up?"

"Just wanted to check when you're going to be home tonight," I say.

"Huh?" he yells.

"When are you going to be home?" I yell back.

"Tonight?"

"Yes!" This is exasperating.

"Uh, not till at least eleven. Oh, sh—!" I hear something clatter in the background. "Babe, I gotta go."

That's all I need to hear. I have until eleven. I throw the car into gear and screech out of my driveway. Looking at the clock on my dashboard, I notice I've wasted four precious minutes on Warren.

Butterflies come up in my stomach as I drive. The familiar feel of the cold sweat dripping down my sides. I can't believe this is real.

Despite my better judgment, at the first stop sign I scroll through my text messages to find the one from Harris. It came in this afternoon, after I'd left to pick up the girls from school.

"Loved having you here today. Want to see you again. Desperately. Come by the house tonight?"

"I'd love to, but I can't get away," I responded.

"Yes, you can. I need you," he wrote.

His forwardness surprised me, but what I had said was true. I really couldn't just up and leave. I have children to take care of.

"I don't have a babysitter for the girls," I responded.

A good fifteen minutes went by without a response, and I figured (with great disappointment) that was the end of it. At least I would get to see him tomorrow at work again. Then a new text came in:

"Hired you a babysitter. Vetted by a nanny agency. Name is Emily. She'll be there by 8:30. Will that work?"

It took me a moment to catch my breath. This amazing man wanted to see me so much that he found me a babysitter? Wow, he's like a knight in shining armor. He must really want to spend time with me tonight.

Of course, I told him I would come. Like Cinderella, though, I have to be back on time. If not, I'll have to explain to Warren where I've been. And I haven't begun to think up a story that he would buy.

But I couldn't pass up the opportunity to be alone with Harris again. I'm tingling with anticipation. What will happen between us tonight?

39

Harris

Dropping my keys on the kitchen table, I look around to make sure the house looks presentable. It's perfect. Paloma does an exceptional job keeping this place looking tidy. She needs a raise. I look in the refrigerator to make sure I have something I can offer Thalia when she arrives. The romantic thing would have been to buy her flowers. I'll ask Iris to send something over next time. White roses, maybe. I think they have some kind of meaning, though I don't know what. Anyway, they're pure and clean, like Thalia.

I'm well-stocked with beverages, but there's very little food in here. Paloma must have had to throw so much of it out that she stopped buying it. For the last few months, I'm out of the house so much I almost never eat here. Before I can worry too much about what to offer my much-anticipated guest, there is a knock at the door. She's here.

As soon as I see her standing under the porch light, my heart feels like it expands three sizes in my chest, warming my whole body. I feel a genuine smile spread across my face, nothing like the flashy one I use all day campaigning.

When I'm with Thalia, I feel like I'm home.

That dinner at her house was a revelation. I've never been in such a loving, warm environment before. The feeling of family, of life, of mischief and fun. And she clearly was the one who created it all. And sustains it all. No matter how comfortable I may have looked, I was completely out of my element that night. My family was so cold, so formal. We love each other, but in an efficient, professional, care-taking way, not a lively, happy, fun one.

I met her a few times back when Cleo and I were together in college, but she was so young then. I didn't even notice her. She's blossomed into an extraordinary woman. Caring, compassionate, and nurturing.

She's the exact opposite of Cleo.

Thalia almost makes me forget about Cleo altogether, which is a welcome thing.

She would be perfect if she wasn't already married to another man.

I know I'm playing with fire, with both her and her sister. But I'm a man who gets what he wants, even when he doesn't know exactly what that is.

I pull Thalia towards me in the living room, circle my arms around her waist, and kiss her lightly on the lips. She smells like gardenia.

She kisses me back, then giggles and holds up a paper bag.

"What is that?" I ask. "Please tell me it's legal."

"Of course," she smiles. "I made you brownies. Legal ones."

I'm touched. Homemade brownies? I don't think my

stepmother ever made homemade brownies in her life.

"Well, let's not let them go to waste. To the kitchen," I say.

"Sit down," she invites me. "Now tell me where I can find the plates."

I can't help comparing this moment to the one where her sister fed me Thai food just a few weeks ago. A very different feeling comes over me at the memory, but I push that thought away.

Before I know it, she's located dessert plates, forks, and glasses. She plates two enormous brownies and sets one in front of me. I don't think I could finish it in this lifetime. And charmingly, she fills two glasses with milk and sets them on the table. I love admiring her supreme comfort in the kitchen. This woman serves, not out of a sense of duty or compulsion, but with a grace and ease that's inspiring to watch.

We sit and gaze at each other across the table, eating her gooey, delicious brownies. For the first time, I realize I have very little to say. For the blink of an eye, I miss Cleo. There's never a dull moment when she's around. But then Thalia's gentle voice breaks in.

"I brought you a gift," she says.

My eyebrows raise, which produces a blush on her cheeks. Her eyes fall to her lap.

"It's nothing much, I just thought…"

"No, it's wonderful," I say. "Where is it?"

She slips into the living room and returns with a small package. "It's from a gallery. It made me think of you…"

I take the package and tear off the paper. The last time I remember doing this was as a child on my birthday. It's a small photo, artistically shot and framed. The image is arresting, painful even. The sad, empty bench is an accurate metaphor for my life.

"Thank you, Thalia. This is very thoughtful."

"I can only stay until ten-thirty or so," she says. "I have to be home before Warren."

That gives us a little over an hour. I don't want to spend the whole time on dessert.

I push my plate forward, get up from my chair, and walk around her side of the table. I take her hand and pull her gently up. Something about her brings out the lamb in me, rather than the lion.

"Come with me," I say, intending to take her to the bedroom. She hasn't been in there before, but it feels like the time is right.

She pulls back for a split second, hesitating.

"We'll just talk," I promise. "Nothing more."

I hope that isn't the truth. But it works. She follows me.

"Come, sit down," I say. She sits on the edge of the bed, perched. She seems unsure how far to let this go. I'll take the lead, but not push her too far.

I kneel down in front of her and take her shoes off. She could use a foot massage. Too bad I'm not into that kind of thing. I make a mental note to ask Iris to buy a spa day for her, along with the flowers.

I take my own shoes off as she watches with the slightest smile. As I'm loosening my tie, I notice something.

The pillows are wrong.

I never wanted all those idiotic throw pillows covering half the bed, but the designer insisted on putting them there. So now every day after I leave, Paloma comes in and makes the bed, throw pillows and all. Every day, she makes it the same way. Huge square pillows in the back, big rectangular pillows in front of them, one square pillow with design in the center, followed by the two small pillows in the very front.

Today, the two small pillows are behind the one square pillow with the design in the center. It's backwards. It's wrong.

Something about this bothers me more than it should. Paloma is excellent. And consistent. She does everything the same way, every single day, just the way I like it.

I tell myself I'm overreacting. All this campaigning has exhausted me. I'm sure Paloma has a reason. Maybe she got interrupted in the middle of making the bed. Phone call or something. Or maybe she just wanted to try something different.

I chastise myself for being such a fool. I know I'm getting overly perfectionist when I'm worried about throw pillows I hate, instead of paying attention to this beautiful woman right in front of me.

Impulsively, I brush all the silly things onto the floor. I lay down on top of the covers and motion for Thalia to join me. She does, and the next thing I know, she is in my arms.

I'm holding her, and smelling her hair, and feeling safer and more secure than I ever have in my life. Which is absurd, because having a married woman in your bed when trying to win an election to a national office is the height of stupidity.

Nevertheless, I put all other thoughts out of my mind. This isn't salacious. It's pure. And lovely. And short-lived.

Before I know it, Thalia has to go home. She has to relieve the babysitter and put things back in order before her husband gets home.

And then I'm sure she'll get in bed with him, just like she was with me, but they'll probably make love before drifting off to sleep.

And I'll be falling asleep alone.

40

Cleo

I can hear the buzz of the refrigerator all the way down the hall in my bedroom. I never noticed that before. It's grating on my nerves. It's keeping me awake.

That buzzing. It's taking over my head.

I can't just lie here staring into the dark.

I can't sleep.

I have to do something.

That's it.

I have to *do* something.

I'm going to rent a car. Nothing will be open now. I don't want to wait until morning. I want to rent a car now. The airport. I can drive down to the airport. But what will I do with my car when I get there? I'll just park it at the airport lot for a few days.

Yes.

I throw back my covers and leap out of bed. Grabbing the nearest jeans and jacket, I dress quickly and grab my bag. I'm off to SeaTac to rent a nondescript vehicle that's untraceable to me. Well, unless you ran the plates or something, but I'll not give anyone a reason to do that.

What a brilliant idea. "Thank you, fridge," I say as I pass the kitchen.

Tomorrow I'll get up early, dress in clothes that don't look like me, and drive an anonymous rental car. I'm going to follow Mr. Harris Cox until I catch him with his whore. I'll find out who this tramp is if it's the last thing I do.

Almost two exhausting hours later, I arrive back at the condo in my dull white rental sedan, blood pumping. I'm going to catch him with her. I don't know where she'll turn up, whether it'll be at an appearance or at his home, but when I see her, I'll know. Maybe she'll ride with him to one of his appearances. Or just meet him there, smiling coquettishly at him. Or touching his tie, or fixing his hair. Maybe she'll meet him at home at the end of the night, drawing him a bath and kissing him in the front room behind the sheers.

Either way, I'll catch her.

And then what will I do? I can't do anything to harm Harris or his career. I'll wait. As long as I know who she is, I can go from there. I'll plot, I'll plan, I'll scheme.

She's going down. No matter who she is.

Evil woman, trying to steal Harris from me. He's mine.

I get back into my bed, pull the covers up to my neck, and smile. I'm taking action. I'm going to make this right. I won't let him slip through my fingers again.

He'll be grateful in the end.

We love each other.

3 Days Before Election Day

41

Harris

There's a hint of femininity lingering in the air. I think it's Thalia's delicate scent on my bed covering. Lying with her in my arms was magical. Sweet. I felt strong and powerful holding her as she melted into me.

It didn't last long enough, seeing as how she had to go home to her husband.

I sit on the edge of my bed and stretch, ridding Thalia from my mind, at least for the time being. I can think about her when I see her. I have important matters to attend to. The election is almost here, and I still have the last few important days of campaigning to get through. Then a win. Hopefully. Polls are tight, but my team assures me we'll be victorious Tuesday night.

That threat is still hanging out there, but I haven't heard any more from whomever left the envelope on the office doorstep. If they were serious, I think they would have contacted me again by now. They would have made a demand; blackmail, or a bribe, or something. But there's been no more communication.

My father's efforts must be paying off. I know he said he didn't think it was Ryan, but I suspect it was. I know how intimidating my father's people can be when they want to. Whatever contact they made with Ryan, it probably scared him enough to drop the whole thing.

I know my father is still convinced Cleo has it in for me, but it can't be her. Despite all her crazy, she loves me. She would never deliberately sabotage me, no matter how angry she was.

I grab my phone to check the latest news. There's a text from my campaign manager. Good news. Internal polls are up from the last count. She's cautiously optimistic that this election will come out in our favor.

The appearance with my father tomorrow should help even more. Dad's always been popular with voters. He's a natural politician, some of which has rubbed off on me, I hope. Appearing with him publicly the weekend before the vote can only help.

Things are looking up. In just a few days I'll be a Congressman-elect, and I can stop worrying so much about my public image. Once I'm elected, no one will care what I do. Elected officials get a surprising pass for indiscretions of the heart. I can pursue Thalia more directly then.

She's so lovely and tender. Maybe the public will even embrace her. After she leaves her husband for me.

42

Cleo

I don't want to get out of the shower. The cold and damp outside seems to have leaked into my home, and into my soul. The only thing that chases away the depression is the hot spray and the clouds of steam. Closing my eyes, I drift off into a soothing reality where everything goes exactly the way it should. No secrets, no lies, no stalking, and no dead children.

Suddenly, I hear a knock. BAM BAM BAM. Someone is at the door? This early? Probably some religious nut. I'm not going to answer it.

Then BAM BAM BAM again.

And again.

BAM BAM BAM BAM BAM.

Insistent.

Whoever is there isn't going to let up.

The pounding in my heart is almost as loud as the pounding on the door. It must be an emergency.

I slam the water off and slide out of the shower. I'm dripping wet and I slip, but catch myself before falling to the ground.

BAM BAM BAM.

BAM BAM BAM BAM BAM.

I'm coming! I shout inside my head.

I wrap the towel around myself and rush to the front door, water cascading from my hair down my back, leaving a slippery trail behind me on the wood floor. I almost slip again, grabbing the doorknob to stop my fall.

No way I'm opening the door to some random strangers, no matter how insistently they knock. I'm not stupid. Nor dressed.

Through the peephole, I see that it's two men in black suits. One of them looks around suspiciously, as if he's checking to make sure they're alone.

The other one speaks. He's tall. "Ms. Tait, we know you're inside. Please open the door. This is official business."

Official? Official what? My only business is teaching at a university. I don't respond, but keep watching them through the hole.

"Ms. Tait. Open the door."

Something in his tone hypnotizes me into opening it. I don't want to, but I feel commanded. Like I don't have a choice.

I unlock it and open the door just a crack, since I'm only wearing a towel. Which is about to fall off, since I can't hold the door open and hide behind it at the same time as holding up the towel.

"Good morning, Ms. Tait," says the tall one. "Do you mind if we come in?"

"Of course I mind," I say. "I don't know who you are. And I almost sprained an ankle running out of the shower to get the door, so I'm feeling a little less than accommodating right now."

"My partner and I have a few questions we need to ask you," he says.

"You can ask your questions right here," I say.

"I think you'll agree that it would be much better to discuss this matter inside," he says. He puts his hand on the door as if he's going to push it in if I say no.

The other guy, who's been preoccupied with looking around until now, sees something that upsets him. He speaks to his partner, as if I'm not there. "We need to get in. Now."

Tall Guy says, "Excuse me, Ms. Tait," as he swiftly pushes the door open. Before I know it, the two of them are inside the living room, and Partner is closing the door and locking it.

"Sit down. Please," says Tall.

I'm genuinely frightened now. Two men have just forced their way into my home, and I almost couldn't be more exposed, standing here in a bath towel that keeps threatening to slip off, dripping wet, and barefoot on a slippery floor. I'm not just going to take this. I'll find a way out. No way in hell these two are getting their hands on me.

I have no idea what they're up to, or what they want. Whatever it is, they're not getting it from me.

But I need clothes and shoes if I'm going to get out of here.

They expect me to be scared. If I act confident, they'll be on their guard, which is exactly what I don't want. I can throw them off by acting like the frightened little woman they want me to be.

"Yes, sir," I say in my most obedient voice. "Would you mind? I mean, could I have permission, please, to put some clothes on first, before you ask me your questions?"

Partner nods his head, and Tall Guy says, "Okay. But make it quick. Forester here is going to accompany you. To make sure you're safe."

I'm sure they're oh-so-concerned with my safety. But I go to my bedroom without asking questions. Forester follows me silently. At least he doesn't follow me into my bedroom, just kind of loiters outside the door. I pin up my soaking hair with a shiver. As I'm putting on my underwear and bra, I ponder my options. Could I get out through the window? It's two floors down. I don't think I could jump. I suppose I could go onto the balcony and scream, but I know at least one of my neighbors doesn't even like me, so I doubt he would do anything other than yell at me to shut up.

Just as I'm buttoning up a pair of jeans, Forester throws open the door and says, "Come on. Now."

He's not fooling around, so I don't either. He's just seen me in my bra, but oh well. I grab the nearest shirt off a hanger and am still buttoning it up as Forester pulls me down the hall by my elbow. I never had the chance to put shoes on.

Forester almost throws me down onto the couch. He's losing his cool. Tall Guy is still professional. He's retrieved a dining chair and pulls it up in front of me.

"I'm sorry we got off on a bad foot. Let me introduce myself, and maybe we can start over. I'm Special Agent Savedra, and this is Special Agent Forester."

I notice they don't bother showing me any badges. Not that I'd know whether they were authentic.

"We're here because we have received information that you've perpetrated a threat against a candidate for U.S. Congress. We need—"

"Is that what this is about?" I ask. "Did Harris send you?" This is absurd.

"Ms. Tait, I'm not at liberty to discuss that. The reason for our visit is to discuss the threat that you made against Mr. Cox." He pulls a digital recorder out of his pocket, turns it on, and sets it on the coffee table in front of me.

"I didn't threaten him. And I don't consent to being recorded in my own home," I say.

I think I detect a slight smirk from Special Agent Tall Guy. Savedra.

"Noted," he says. He doesn't move to turn off the recording device. "Ms. Tait, we know about the threatening note you left for Candidate Cox. We know you delivered it to his campaign office sometime on the evening of October 30."

I don't respond, and I try not to show any emotion on my face.

"It's important," he says, "for national security, that you confess to delivering the document to Mr. Cox's office."

"I'm not confessing anything to you. Aren't you supposed to at least offer me a lawyer before interrogating me?"

"Ms. Tait, let's not play games here. We know you were involved in a hit-and-run car accident in 2003, causing the death of a child. We also know that you are attempting to frame Harris Cox for said accident."

"This is absurd!" This statement has got me on my toes now. I've got to be sharp to get past these guys. I have to be very careful with my choice of words. "You've broken into my home against my will, despite the fact that I was undressed. You're essentially holding me hostage, and now you're accusing me of framing Harris for some crime I know nothing about?" That was good.

"Let's not start throwing accusations around, Ms. Tait. We deal only in the truth."

"Right," I snort.

"You were in the vehicle that hit and subsequently caused the death of the young girl, correct?" Savedra says. I don't respond. He turns the recorder off. "For your own good, I would like you to answer that question. Aloud. I don't want to escalate this interview any further than I have to." He turns the recorder back on. "Now, you were about to state whether you were in the vehicle that hit the young girl in 2003."

He gives Forester, who's standing behind me, a look that terrifies me. All of a sudden, I remember Ryan telling me about the guys in the black SUV following him. These must be the same guys. Who is putting them up to this? I don't think they actually hurt Ryan, just freaked him out pretty good. They won't make me their victim. I'll turn the tables on them first.

"Who sent you goons here?" I ask. "You think I'm going to fall for your little scam? You can't just come to my home and intimidate me into making some false confession on tape. Get out of here, now, before I scream and half the building calls the police."

Forester is pissed off now. He storms around to the front of the couch, grabs me by the throat, and pushes me back against the seat. "Shut up, little woman," he says. "Do you think this is a game? We have proof that you were there. Admit it now and maybe you can save yourself some trouble."

"What proof?" I choke out.

"A bloody yellow dress," he says. "Does that ring a bell?"

Oh god, these guys are for real. They have the dress. Why did I let Mary drive away with it that day? I should have taken it home myself and burned the damn thing.

"Okay, okay," I say. "What do you want?"

Forester lets up on my throat. Savedra answers, "All we're here to do is to ensure the safety of Mr. Cox, who, as you know, is a prominent public figure against whom a serious threat has been made." He smiles. "And that we can prove," he adds.

I take a deep breath. I can't admit to anything. How am I going to get out of this?

I stall. "What exactly do you think you can prove?"

"That you were driving the car on September 24, 2003 on Forest Road 46, and that you hit the young female and drove away, causing her subsequent death. And that you were alone."

"How could you possibly prove any of that? Even if you could prove I was there, how could you prove I was alone?"

"We have our ways, Ms. Tait. Enough screwing around. This is your last chance. If you refuse, we will be forced to take more serious precautions to protect Senator Cox's reputation." He shoves the recorder in front of me. I grab it and speak directly into it.

"My name is Cleo Tait. Today is November 3, 2018. At approximately eight o'clock this morning, two presumably armed men broke into and entered my home without my consent. I was undressed at the time. They proceeded to interrogate me without providing any legitimate identification or access to an attorney. They have accused me, threatened me, and refused to leave my home. They identified themselves as Special Agents Savedra and Forester, which may or may not be their real names. Fortunately, they've left their fingerprints all over my condo, so their true identities can be learned when the police arrive to investigate their attempted kidnapping and possible assault." I smirk at them, shove the recorder back across the table, and scream in my best helpless female voice, "Help! Help! Rape!!"

Savedra swears under his breath. He scoops up the recorder, and he beats a path to the door like his pants are on fire. Forester follows right behind.

I win for today, but I have a feeling this is just the beginning.

43

Harris

The barista places the tiny espresso cup on the marble countertop in front of me, jolting me back into reality. My mind has been elsewhere all morning. I feel my politician smile flash across my face automatically, noticing how phony it is. But that first sip of espresso... It's the only thing that gets me out of bed some days. I sip the crema off the top before even walking away from the counter. Two blissful minutes later, I'm chasing my shot with some water, and it's time to get back to real life.

On cue, my father calls. "I don't have long to chat, son, but I want to touch base and make sure everything is set for the joint appearance tomorrow."

"As far as I know, Iris has everything handled. She and Mary have been in constant contact," I say. "You're taking care of the speeches, right?"

"Yes, I've asked Aaron to write something out for both of us."

"Good," I say as I unlock my car and slide in. "Have him text it to me so I can take a look at it—"

"I don't have a lot of time, son, but we need to discuss the more pressing matters," he interrupts. I was hoping to avoid this. I gulp.

"Sure, Dad, go ahead," I say.

"We're proceeding forward with the investigation, and we've run into a bit of trouble."

"I told you it was Ryan. I thought you had scared him off and we could let it go. After all, I haven't heard any more from whomever left the envelope at the office," I say. "Surely we have more important things to worry about this close to the election."

"Son, you must understand. Under no uncertain terms has this threat been eliminated. Someone out there has incriminating information about you and has threatened to use it. Winning the election will not change that. We must positively identify the threat and eliminate it. It is imperative."

"Dad..."

"Imperative," he says. "Son, how do you think I've lasted this long in politics? By being a good boy? By ignoring my enemies? Or by ruthlessly crushing them preemptively whenever they poked their heads out of the sand? I think you know the answer to that. You've known that answer since you were a child. Don't start pleading naiveté now. You're in this up to your eyeballs, and you're never going to get out. This is politics. This is power. Use it or be used by it. Period."

For the first time, I think I may regret following in my father's footsteps. Yes, I've always known my father had to take extraordinary steps to get where he is, and I've benefitted from that. But I don't think I ever wanted to face the truth of what that really meant. The people I'd have to betray and the lives I'd have to ruin. I feel sick. But he's right, there's no way out now.

I am who I have become.

"So what do you want from me, Dad?" I know how weary I sound compared to his commanding energy.

"You already know about the team I sent to interrogate the boyfriend. And I've just spoken with the agents who called on Ms. Tait this morning."

"You sent people to her?" I ask. "Tell me she wasn't harmed."

"Unfortunately, things didn't go as planned. Ms. Tait was uncooperative, to say the least."

"What happened, Dad? What did they do to her?" I swallow, forcing nightmare scenarios out of my mind.

"The agents attempted to extract a confession out of her, admitting that she was the driver and sole occupant of the vehicle the day of the accident."

"But she wasn't."

"For our purposes, she was," says Dad. "She decided unwisely to make a scene and so the agents were forced to leave without getting what they needed. Which makes it all the more necessary that we take this operation to the next level."

"Meaning...?" I ask.

"I'm assuming that you've done as I asked regarding Mrs. Edwards."

"Well, she is working for me now as an assistant. I'm not sure what else you want me to do with her."

"I was hoping it wouldn't have to come to this, but we're going to need some blackmail material. She appears not to have any vices we can exploit, other than perhaps yourself."

"No, Dad, I told you—"

"Yes." This is clearly not going to be optional. "I've had a reservation made for you tonight at the Edgewater

Hotel. You are to bring her there under some pretense, and get her into a compromising position, if you understand my meaning. The room will be set up in advance with cameras to record your interactions."

"For what purpose?" I ask. This is madness. I won't do it.

"Incentive," he says. "As far as we can tell, she is a dedicated family woman. She won't want her family destroyed."

"Dad!" I've had enough now. Thalia has nothing to do with any of this. I don't even understand why she has to be involved. "Enough! This cockamamie plan isn't even logical. What does blackmailing Thalia have to do with anything?"

My father sighs. He is exasperated with me. In a measured tone which barely conceals his anger, he says, "Mrs. Edwards is the only family that your Cleo has. Ms. Tait has also recently gifted her sister with a large sum of money, which indicates that she must care about her deeply."

He pauses. I suppose to let my own stupidity sink in.

"Leverage," he says. "We need leverage against Cleo. She's strong-willed and could prove a problem in the future if we don't subdue her now. We need to force a taped confession out of her, admitting to driving the car the day of the accident. And if she won't do it for her own best interest, perhaps she will do it to save her beloved sister's unfaithfulness from being exposed in sordid fashion to the world."

"So you want a sex tape," I say.

"They never fail," says Dad.

I always looked up to my dad. I thought he was a genius. He magically made things go his way. I thought it was because he was so charismatic, because people loved him and wanted to get on board with his great ideas. Am I to realize now that he's done everything in the dirtiest of all possible fashions? Despicable.

I want no part of this anymore. Not politics, not even the election. But it's too late to get out. The election is in three days. I almost wish I could lose.

But all the fight is drained out of me right now.

"Okay, Dad," I say. "I'll do it."

44

Cleo

I don't make stupid decisions. I'm impulsive, maybe even rash. It's part of my charm.

But writing that threatening note and dropping it off at Harris's office may have been legitimately stupid.

Those two thugs have been gone for over an hour, and I'm still shaking. I'm proud of the way I handled myself, but I don't know what I've gotten myself into. Whatever it is, I'm in deep.

I pace my living room, brooding over the events of the morning.

Whoever Savedra and Forester are, no way they're actual law enforcement. No badges or uniforms, and their conduct was highly unorthodox. Probably even illegal.

Obviously, they were here about Harris. He has really gotten paranoid since he got the note. Maybe I should just call him and smooth the whole thing over. Admit that I wrote the damned thing when I was upset.

Once he knows it was me, he can call off his goons and leave me alone.

The thought of talking to Harris warms me, but I don't get too attached to it. I swore I wouldn't do that. The reason I went out last night to get the rental car was to go undercover and do some sleuthing. Before I talk to him again, I want to know exactly what — and who — I'm dealing with. Who is this other woman and what are his intentions with her?

The phone call idea is a no go.

There's something nagging at me about those two guys. Something I just can't put my finger on. What is it? Something they said.

The moment they said they were going to be forced to escalate the situation to protect Harris...

Wait a minute. That's it. They didn't say Harris. They said they were going to protect the *Senator's* reputation. Oh my god, that's it.

The Senator is behind this.

Of course. He's always had some kind of sinister infrastructure for making problems go away. Fifteen years ago, an innocent child died because he covered it up. And now I've provoked this powerful man into hounding first Ryan, and now me.

This is far worse than I thought.

Senator Cox has been the burr in my side for fifteen years. He's ruined my life, and he is well past any ability to negotiate with. Going against him is beyond stupid. It's dangerous.

I'm in over my head.

I've experienced the breadth of the Senator's influence before, but I have no idea the depth of his power. Do I really have what it takes to stand up to him?

This all started because Harris needed me. That day in the hospital was so perfect. I should have let things be as they were, but I just had to spy on him. I had to let my jealousy get the better of me. Planting that envelope was playing with fire. What an unbelievable fool I was to think I could get revenge on Harris. To win against a powerful political dynasty-in-the-making.

There's no sense in punishing myself now. Or wallowing in self-pity. It's time to take stock of the situation and make a plan to go forward.

So I planted the threat at Harris's office. His father somehow seems to have figured out it was me and sent thugs to force a false confession out of me about the accident. That way, if the accident is ever revealed, it will look like it's my fault, not Harris's.

The way I see it, I have two choices. Either give in to the Senator's demands, or fight back.

My instincts are going to win out. I'm a fighter.

But I need a plan.

Senator Cox is desperate to pin the accident on me. He claims to have my dress as evidence. I have to prove that I wasn't the one driving the car, but how can I? The only thing I have from that day is the photo of Harris and me at the lake in the afternoon.

I get excited for a brief second when I remember that the date is printed right on the photo. But just as quickly, I shut myself down. Even if the printed date couldn't be debunked, all it proves is that we were at the lake that day together. It doesn't exonerate me, or even show that I wasn't the driver.

All of a sudden, it hits me. If I kept the photo from that day, maybe Harris has kept mementos of his own. I fire up my laptop to check his schedule of appearances. Bingo. He's knocking on doors all morning over in Ballard. I should have until at least noon.

I hop in the rental car and speed over to Harris's house. The back door is unlocked, just like before. I don't have long, but I shouldn't need much time. If there's anything useful in here — photos, a journal — it shouldn't take long to find it. He keeps the place so tidy.

I'm not sure what I'm looking for, but I figure I'll know it when I see it. I take a good look around and make a plan of attack. I'll start with the rooms I've already been in, since I should be able to knock those out quick. First, the bedroom. It's a lot messier than last time. The bed is unmade and there are clothes on the floor. I paw through them and see that they're only Harris's. No women's clothing. Just to make sure.

Working fast, I search the drawers, the closet, and under the bed. Nothing unusual there. Nor in the bathroom cabinets. Nothing here looks like it could hold fifteen-year-old mementos. It doesn't look like there's anything over a year old in the whole house.

Next the living room. Behind and under the furniture is clear. I peek behind the curtains, even though it's pointless. Those horrible gray sheers flash back a memory of Harris kissing someone else through them. I push the image out of my mind.

The clock on the living room wall ticks. Loud. Urgent. Goading me on.

To the coat closet. It's nothing but a bunch of coats and an unused umbrella on the top shelf.

Tick. Tick. Tick.

Hurry, before Harris gets home.

What did his schedule say? Do I have until noon? I thought so, but now I'm not sure.

Tick. Tick.

I can't let him find me here.

Tick.

Skip the kitchen.

Tick.

Go straight to the office.

Tick.

Should have started here first.

Breathe, Cleo. My hand shakes as I twist the knob and push open the door.

The office is as pristine as the rest of the house. I sigh. Has he scrubbed every trace of life away? This is the home of a man with no history. No family, no love. Maybe that's just it. No history equals no secrets.

Hopelessness washes over me, but I press on. I will leave no stone unturned.

The desk holds only typical office supplies: pens, paper, stapler, paper clips, and some other odds and ends. But the filing cabinet. I bet that's the jackpot.

I'm surprised to find it's locked, considering his carelessness with his back door. But I'm not deterred. Where would he keep the key? I check the desk again. It's not in plain sight in the drawer. I lift out the removable pencil tray and what do you know, there it is. He's not very good at this. Clearly, he needs my help.

File cabinet open, I rifle through the manila folders. All meticulously marked. This should be easy.

Most of these look to be related to his law practice. Until I get to the bottom drawer, way in the back. A folder marked September 24, 2003. This is it.

My heart beats so hard I can hear blood pumping in my ears. I collapse on the floor, hesitating. I don't know what I'm going to find. The folder is old and beat up, with random numbers scribbled on it. You'd think he'd use a nicer folder for one of the most important things that ever happened to him.

To us.

My fingers run down the edge of the folder and slip behind the top layer. I take a deep breath and ease it open.

It's empty.

It feels like a gut punch. I'm devastated. Whatever documents he may have once had, they're gone now. Shredded, burned, who knows? Why would he keep this tattered folder but destroy its contents?

I may never understand this man.

Silently cursing him, I put everything back the way I found it, lock the cabinet, and return the key to the desk. This trip was an utter waste. I've found nothing to help me prove I wasn't the driver of the car. And I've missed my opportunity to tail Harris all morning.

Now I just have to get out of here before he returns home.

Down the hall.

Through the living room.

Tick. Tick. Tick.

I hustle.

CLICK.

I freeze.

SCRAPE.

Someone is unlocking the front door.

Oh, no.

I'm going to get caught.

I can't let that happen. So I do the first thing I can think of. I dive into the coat closet and silently close the door. Huddled on the floor under Harris's long wool coats, I listen. I hear a woman's voice. She's speaking under her breath, as if to herself. Could this be the other woman? The one he's cheating on me with?

I want to burst through the door, shove her to the ground, and pummel her unconscious, but I suppress the urge.

Instead, I listen. Straining to hear through the door. Her voice sounds… too old to be dating Harris. Some plastic bags rustle. Then the lid of the kitchen trash slams shut.

I exhale with relief. It must be his maid. She's here to clean up, take out the trash. That explains why his bedroom was a mess. She probably comes in every morning after he leaves. If I just wait, she'll eventually go. I wonder how long that will take?

It's uncomfortable scrunched up on the floor in this hot, stuffy closet. I try to shift position without making a sound, and I smack my hand on something metal. I have to stifle myself from crying out. It's pitch black in here so I can't see, but I feel around to find out what I just hit.

It's a safe. With a combination lock.

I didn't see it before because it's at the back of the closet, hidden behind the long coats.

This is big.

The safe doesn't budge. It must be bolted down. This is what I've been looking for. I can feel it. Now how do I get the combination?

Ms. Maid is vacuuming now. This could take a while. I have to get out of here before Harris gets back, so I'm trying not to panic. I can't hear the ticking of that clock over the roar of the vacuum, but I can feel it beating in my heart. I'm getting more and more nervous about the time, but I can't take a chance on trying to escape without her seeing me. I'll have to wait it out.

I spin the lock around a few times on the safe, halfway hoping that I'll accidentally open it. Idiotic visions of drugging Harris and forcing him to reveal it to me go through my mind until it hits me. How stupid could I be? The scribbling on the folder. It's the combination.

I can hardly wait for the maid to get out of here, and the

minute I hear the scrape of the key in the front lock, I'm out of the closet like a shot. No way I'm going to miss this opportunity. Back in the office, I reopen the cabinet, retrieve the folder, and memorize the scribbled numbers. Once I put everything back meticulously in its place, I go to the closet and try the safe. It opens on the first try.

I'm shaking with nerves. Harris could be back any minute. But I'm so close I can't give up now.

Inside the safe is a stack of papers. The usual stuff, like a passport, birth certificate, and social security card. Titles to his house and car, and some financial statements with numbers big enough to raise my eyebrows. I knew Harris's family was well off, but nine figures? I don't have time to obsess over that now, though. There's also a large envelope, which holds a few original copies of the newspaper articles about the accident, as well as an information file about the family of the little girl. A pang of guilt stabs me, but I have to move on. I'm getting warmer.

Under all the papers is a small metal case. It looks so much like the one that burgundy skirt-suited woman threw my dress into... but it couldn't be. Harris wouldn't have that box. It's locked, with a key this time. There's no getting into this one.

Then I see it. The one last thing in this safe. A tiny, polished wooden box. I open it up and gasp at the sight of a gorgeous, sparkling diamond ring. It's huge. Jealousy and rage flood my whole body. He's going to marry her? This woman he's cheating on me with? That will never happen, no matter what I have to do.

As soon as I get the Senator's goons off my back, I will find out who she is and get rid of her altogether.

I want so badly to take this ring, but I can't bring myself to do it. He'd definitely notice it. But this ugly metal box? I'm taking it. I'll figure out how to get it open later.

45

Thalia

My feet are killing me after walking all over Ballard with Harris this morning. I shouldn't have worn heels. What was I thinking? I guess I was trying to look good. That was a big mistake, judging by the size of the blisters forming on my toes.

But at least Harris and I are sitting down for a quick lunch before heading back out again. I've never eaten in a private dining room before. It's much quieter than sitting across the table from Warren and the kids at a germ-infested pizza and games establishment. I feel so sophisticated when I'm with Harris. Actually, the truth is I feel like I'm acting sophisticated, while never really fitting in.

A niggling little feeling is growing in the pit of my stomach. The harder I try to ignore it, the stronger it seems to get. I don't know what to call it. Guilt? Fear? I sneak a little extra-long gaze at Harris, appreciating his strong, capable presence. I am enamored, that is for sure. But who wouldn't be? Rich, gorgeous, soon-to-be powerful politician shows an interest in a housewife. Am I fooling myself? Why is he doing this, anyway? What could he possibly see in me?

"How do you like the sablefish?" he asks, calling me back to reality.

"I've never eaten this before," I say, not sure how to answer. I'd much rather be eating a turkey sandwich with chips and a soda, but I can't possibly admit that. Just before I'm forced to come up with something clever to say, my phone rings.

"Excuse me, I'm so sorry," I say to Harris.

"Of course, go ahead," he obliges. He's the perfect gentleman, as always. I smile.

I look at the caller ID. It's Warren. Uh-oh.

"Hi, hon," I say. "I can't really —"

"Where the hell are you, Thalia?" he demands. The girls are screaming at each other in the background. He's fuming.

"Um —"

"I'm supposed to be at the restaurant right now, and I have two twin girls here who need a mother. I'll ask you again, where the hell are you?"

I wince, knowing Harris can at least hear Warren's tone of voice, if not the words as well. Attempting a modicum of privacy, I turn away and put my hand over my mouth.

"What about the nanny? Emily? She was supposed to be there at noon. Didn't she show?" I ask, half under my breath.

"Speak up, Thalia! You wanted me to fix this restaurant, begged me to fix it, but in order to do that, I have to BE THERE! I don't give a damn about a nanny, Emma-whatever-the-hell, these children need their mother. Get here, from wherever you are, NOW."

And he slams down the phone.

I'm left empty. Empty-handed, empty-headed, I don't know, everything.

Harris is staring at me, motionless, napkin poised in midair. What have I done? I'm sure he heard that entire conversation. Warren was so loud the people two tables over could have heard it. I've never been so embarrassed.

Suddenly, the only thing that's clear to me is that I have to go take care of my children. I have to get home to my family. Everything I've been doing is wrong.

I push away from the table. "I can't do this," I say. "I have to go home." The awkwardness of my abrupt departure hangs in the air, but it's just the truth. I have to go.

Harris stands up, too. "No, Thalia, please don't go. I need you. The campaign needs you." He sounds so hollow.

All I can think about is my family. My children, and yes, even my slovenly husband. He does work hard, after all. I've failed them. What an immature, silly fool I've been. I grab my handbag and turn to leave.

"Stay." Harris seizes my arm. "I'm your boss. You can't leave."

"I guess I have to quit." He doesn't budge. He looks somehow... afraid. Strange. But I don't have time to think about that now. I have to get home to fix my family before it's too late.

I try to pull away, but he doesn't let go.

"Take your hand off me," I say. Slowly, and with as much confidence as I can muster. "I quit."

His hand falls from my arm, and I head towards the door. Just as I grasp the handle, he says, "Can't we at least talk about this? I understand if you have to leave... but can you at least come back tomorrow?"

He sounds desperate. It isn't like him.

I hesitate. "I'm sorry. I just can't," I say.

"Why don't you at least meet me later tonight for a drink? I'll treat you, as a goodbye and thank you sort of... celebration. Please."

Against my better judgment, I tell him I'll think about it.

46

Cleo

I massage the back of my neck with one hand as I control the steering wheel with the other. It's not helping. My stress level is spiraling upward, despite the fact that I escaped Harris's house without getting caught.

The election is in three days, and I'm terrified. My mind keeps slipping back to this morning. I know the Senator sent Savedra and Forester to my condo to force a false confession out of me. I got rid of them, but I'd be a fool to think they're not already working on Plan B to frame me for the accident.

If I can't find something — anything — to prove I wasn't driving the car that day…

Damn Harris. Why is he letting his father do this to me?

My only hope is this metal box. It's sitting in the passenger seat next to me, like an obedient pet dog. As soon as I get home, I'm going to break it open. With a hammer, if I have to. I'm dying to know what's inside it. I really, really need it to be something miraculous.

The other thing I really, really need is to find out who

Harris's other woman is. Two visits, or should I say break-ins, to his house have revealed no additional information on her identity. The memory of that stunning diamond ring makes me nauseous. If I don't put a stop to this relationship, the next time I see that ring, it may be on some other woman's finger.

I can't let that happen.

My eyes blur as a strange feeling overtakes me. I swerve the car off the road and slam on the parking brake. I try to catch my breath, but I'm hyperventilating. Hot tears sting my eyes. I'm losing him again. This time, it will be forever. Sorrow grips my heart and squeezes like a vise. Sobs swell and grow from somewhere deep inside me, escaping my throat with a roar.

This is heartbreak.

This is love.

The force of it has breached the dam holding back my weakness, my vulnerability.

Life without Harris would be unlivable. I don't accept it.

I swipe at my tears, rubbing my eyes hard enough to see stars. Heartache is nothing in the face of sheer determination. I push my hair away from my face and roll my shoulders back. I can handle this.

Aside from tailing Harris, which is easier said than done, I'm out of ideas as to how to find out who his other woman is. He's all over the place in the city, and I don't know how to follow him without getting noticed, even in the rental car. I can't afford to make a scene. So I'll table that goal for today.

In that case, my first step is to put in place a new strategy. If I can't separate him from her, then I will make him so jealous he won't be able to see straight. Tomorrow is his joint appearance rally with his father. I need to bring a date. But who could I bring? The only person in the world I can think of who would come with me on such short notice is Ryan. I'll have a lot of groveling to do, but it will be worth it.

I gather up my courage and call him, inviting myself over to his apartment. A month ago, I would never have dared to jeopardize my career by meeting him there, but I'm long past worrying about such mundane things. It's do or die time.

On the drive, I'm thinking about this metal case. What if Harris finds out it's gone? If he even goes into that safe for one second, for any reason, including God forbid to get out that ring, he'll notice right away that the case is missing. And who will he blame? The maid? I doubt anyone else goes into that place except for her, considering how spotless it is. Well, and *her*. The other woman. Is there some way I could find to blame her for it? Frame her for stealing? Difficult, considering I know nothing about her.

The only smart thing to do would be to turn around right now and put the case back. The door's still unlocked. He won't be home yet, I don't think. That would be the smart move. But who am I kidding? I have to know what's in this box. It could be the exact thing I've been looking for. The sooner I can get it open, the better.

And now for Ryan. What am I going to tell him? How in the world am I going to sweet talk him into taking me back after the way I treated him? I know he hasn't gotten over me; maybe he'll be eager. He did say he loves me. That's it. Maybe I could tell him I'm sorry for everything I said and the heartless way I broke up with him. And that I've realized I love him, too... and maybe add that I want to think about a future with him. Add on marriage, even.

Which reminds me of that damned ring. I can't stand this. I feel my foot pressing down on the accelerator as I tense with anger. Who is this woman? I have to find her. I have to find her. I have to find her. And kill her.

No. Stop it. I'm letting my anger run away with me. I take a deep breath and let it out slowly. No one is going to be killing anyone.

This is Harris's fault. Maybe the other woman is innocent. She might not even know I exist. She's probably a wonderful woman. Which is utterly meaningless if she accepts Harris's proposal. That makes her my mortal enemy.

Then again, Harris doesn't usually fall for the "wonderful woman" type. I should know. What is he doing with her? He should be with me. He knows that. How can he throw away everything we've been through together?

It's his father. The Senator. Again. He's the real villain here. That's where I should focus my anger, not on my beloved Harris. Damn that evil old man, he has single-handedly ruined my entire life. That old lowlife needs to die. I wonder if there's any way I could make that happen and get away with it?

Okay, this has to stop. I'm seriously contemplating what I'm sure is a federal crime complete with death penalty, assassinating a U.S. Senator. But I'd be an assassin, so there is that. Sounds thrilling. But no. I've got to get myself under control.

I can do this. I can get Harris back. I just have to focus. Concentrate. Think.

Go see Ryan. Get him to forgive you. And take you to Harris's rally tomorrow.

47

Harris

No, no, no. Thalia is gone. I can't get through the rest of this miserable day without her.

And what will my father say? I'm such a child. I'm afraid of my father and I'm treating Thalia like she's the mother I wish I had.

I'll text her and see if she'll meet me at the Edgewater. Please, please.

I don't know whether I want her to come because I want to see her, or because my father told me to. Why would I want to lure this perfectly lovely woman to a hotel so I can coerce her into a compromising position and then videotape it in order to blackmail her corrupt sister, whom she loves and trusts implicitly?

Why would I do that? I like Thalia. Or I love her.

Baiting a woman so you can make a sex tape to blackmail her sister is definitely not love.

I am sick.

So is my father.

I'll never get out of this loop.

I text her. "Thalia, meet me for dinner at the Edgewater Hotel. Tonight, 8:00 p.m. To thank you for all you've done for me."

I am sick.

2 Days Before Election Day

48

Cleo

Big day today, so I'm up before the sun. My reunion with Ryan last night went better than planned. I apologized for the way I'd behaved, and for not taking his fears about the stalkers seriously enough. He told me a long, boring story about how the girl he went out with on Halloween turned out to be a nightmare. I flirted just enough to titillate him, then said I wasn't ready to get romantic just yet, but that I would like to back everything up and work on a good solid friendship, no strings attached.

Ryan was more than enthusiastic, and was thrilled I asked him to accompany me downtown today. I didn't tell him it was for Harris's political rally. He'll find out soon enough.

Before I pick Ryan up, though, I have something else pressing to attend to.

This box.

What do I do with it? It's practically burning a hole in my coffee table. I'm desperate to know what's inside. I strongly suspect that whatever it is would be just the thing to get me out of this mess with the Senator's goons following me around and terrorizing me. But it's locked. I have no way to get into it.

Part of me says that the smartest thing would be to skip the rally altogether, and use the time to sneak back in to Harris's place — for the last time — and put the box back in his safe. Then I could wash my hands clean of the whole thing and go on my way.

But it's not that simple. The Senator has it out for me, and I have no choice but to protect myself. It's him or me in this fight. And it sure as hell isn't going to be me.

I'm going to need an extra cup of coffee this morning. After setting the machine on to brew, I sit down to examine the box. I pick it up, turn it over, shake it. There's definitely something inside, but I can't tell what it is. Definitely nothing metal.

Though it's securely locked, the box itself doesn't seem very sturdy. It's lightweight and kind of cheap, like a cash box you could pick up at any local office store. If only I knew how to pick a lock. I'd try bobby pins, but I don't even own any.

I set it down, look at it, turn it around, and think.

I head in to the kitchen to fix my coffee, and when I'm done, I bring the mug back to my seat on the couch. "How do I open you, box?"

Gazing at it intently, as if I can burn it open with my eyes, I slowly stir my coffee.

That's it. The spoon. No, not a spoon. A knife.

I jump up and grab a thin paring knife from a kitchen drawer and wedge it between the top and bottom of the box, a couple of inches over from the lock. It goes right in, lifting that side of the box lid. It's still securely fastened, so I jimmy it around a few times until I realize how the locking mechanism works. All I need to do is maneuver the knife blade so that I can turn the back of the lock a half-turn, and it will unlatch. It takes me a good few minutes, but finally, POP.

The box is open.

And…

It's a plastic bag.

I illegally entered Harris Cox's home, cracked his safe, and made off with a plastic grocery bag.

But I pull the bag out, and it is most definitely *not* empty. My heartbeat quickens with excitement. What am I going to find? I suck in a deep breath. I'm not even sure I'm ready for this. Gingerly, I peel the bag open. The plastic has gone brittle, and breaks apart where some of the creases are. It's obviously been crumpled in this exact position for a long time.

Then I see it.

Oh. My. God.

It's the bloody yellow dress.

It's old, and the blood is brown and crusty and cracked.

At the bottom of the bag is a little old crumpled receipt. And by some miracle, it's still legible. It's the credit card receipt for everything that was bought that day, including the clothes and shoes all in my size, signed by the Senator's very own personal assistant.

I've got him.

This is going to be a fun day.

49

Harris

It's only an hour until the rally, and I am being driven over to Westlake Center in the car Dad hired for me. He's going to meet me there. I'm reading over the speech I'm supposed to give for what feels like the hundredth time. Since the collapse, I've minimized my public speaking as much as I could get away with, and I'm deathly anxious about today. With my dad here, this is going to get a lot of press attention. I've got to get this right. In order to close the deal on this election, total perfection is required.

I have to win. Dad will kill me if I don't.

The driver stops at Westlake, where I'm met by security as I disembark. Iris is with the two guards, and leads me to the backstage area where my dad is waiting. He claps me on the back heartily and says, "Well, son, you ready for this? Let's get this election signed, sealed, and delivered today."

"Of course, Dad," I say, sounding far more confident than I feel.

We go over the agenda for the rally: speeches, Q&A

from the audience, etc. Then my father asks everyone to leave so he and I can have a few moments alone. His demeanor immediately changes. Gone is the jovial, charismatic politician and out comes the serious, intimidating authoritarian.

"Where is Mrs. Edwards?" he asks. "I expected her to be here with you."

"Thalia? She, uh, couldn't make it today. Family obligations…" I offer lamely. He is not amused.

"You know there's no place for that in politics," he says. My father sometimes loses sight of the fact that not everything in the world revolves around election cycles.

"Certainly you accomplished last night's goal," he says. I think I detect the hint of a threat in his tone, but I brush it off.

"No, I'm sorry, I didn't," I say. The muscles in his jaw bulge as he grits his teeth. "I invited her to meet me at the Edgewater, and I waited all night, but she never showed."

His voice rises as he says, "And where is she today? The *truth*."

I can't hide it forever. I might as well admit it.

"She quit."

My father raises his fist as if he's about to smash something, but then gets control of himself and lowers it back down. A slow, controlled exhale escapes from him, and his eyes bore into me. "This is unacceptable. We need that tape. I'm not sure you understand the seriousness of this situation."

"I do," I say. He is stronger than me. I can't fight against him or try to beat him at his own game.

"Tonight," he commands. "You absolutely must carry out this plan tonight. You must."

"Yes," I sigh. "I'll do it."

He doesn't relax much when I say that, but I can't offer any more. The truth is, I don't know whether I'll go through with it. That would entail begging Thalia to meet me at the Edgewater, which I'm not keen to do since I already tried that yesterday and got rejected. And even if I texted her, there's no guarantee she would show up. The whole idea makes me feel sick just thinking about it.

I'll go back to the Edgewater tonight and just wait for her. If she shows up, then I'll carry out my father's twisted plan. If she doesn't, then I guess I'll just have to deal with my father.

I have a few moments alone to practice my speech before the rally begins. Before I'm even two sentences in, I feel my throat seizing up and my lips quivering. This speech is doomed. I can't do it. My stress level is so high with everything going on, I just can't. I start to spiral downward mentally. I see myself out there in front of all those people, most of whom are there to see the Senator, not me. I'll freeze. Just looking at the words on this page in front of me, the letters swim before my eyes. Time slows down, and I feel the tunnel vision setting in. I have to sit down before I faint again.

My jacket pocket buzzes, shocking me back to reality. I shake my head to clear my vision and pull out my phone. It's a text.

From Cleo.

"I'll be there for you today. A friendly face to cheer you on."

This is highly unexpected, but somehow welcome. I feel better knowing at least one of the Tait sisters will be nearby.

50

Cleo

My hand shakes as I unlock the door to my office. The building is deserted, but my head darts from side to side anyway, confirming that I haven't been followed. The second the lock releases, I fall into the room, securing the door behind me.

I'm safe. For now.

Ryan is expecting me to pick him up in forty-five minutes. No way I'll make it on time, but I had no choice. This couldn't wait. I slide my handbag off my shoulder and stash it in the bottom drawer of my desk, checking its contents one more time.

The yellow dress, credit card receipt, and photograph of Harris and me at the lake are still inside.

As soon as I found them in the metal box, I knew I needed a safe place to keep them. Immediately. I can't take a chance at hiding them in my condo. If Harris opens his safe for any reason, he's going to notice the box is missing. The Senator will send his goons over to ransack my place, and I'll lose the only leverage I have over him.

My first idea was to get a safe deposit box at a bank, but that's impossible since it's the weekend. I don't trust banks, anyway. I needed a better solution.

They say the best place to hide things is in plain sight.

So after taking photos of the dress and receipt, I placed them in a large handbag, along with the photo of Harris and me at the lake that day. And a big pair of scissors.

I figured the items would be safe in my office, no matter the time of day or night. Campus Security is always on patrol, and there are cameras everywhere. Breaking and entering my office on a university campus may be a more high-profile affair than even the Senator would want to attempt.

I yank a Psych 401 textbook off my bookshelf. The fattest textbook I have. One of several copies I keep in my office. With my big scissors, I start cutting out pages. About two inches from the binding, I cut straight through from bottom to top, a few pages at a time. Ten minutes later, I'm still cutting. I'm barely even halfway through, and my hands are killing me. But I can't stop. I resort to cutting thick stacks of pages out, even though my hands look like they're about to bleed.

When all the pages are cut out, I have what I wanted. A pristine-looking book cover that's empty on the inside. Now for the final step. I insert the receipt and the photo into an envelope, which I tape to the inside cover of the book. Then I fold the yellow dress into a tiny little bundle and tuck it into the book, where the pages should be. Carefully, carefully, I re-shelve the book. It fits snugly between the other identical copies.

Standing back, I survey my handiwork. The corner of my mouth curls up and a grin spreads across my face. I couldn't be prouder. It's perfect. No one could ever suspect that anything is hidden in here.

Not only have I clawed back the yellow dress from the Senator, I've got his assistant's credit card receipt showing she bought me a new set of clothes that day.

He doesn't know it yet, but he's empty-handed. He no longer has evidence to prove I was at the scene of the accident.

But I do have something on him. Maybe that credit card receipt doesn't exactly prove that the Senator initiated the cover-up, but it's enough to raise questions. He can't try to pin the crime on me without casting suspicion on his own involvement.

I scoop up the hundreds of cut-out pages and shove them into the handbag, along with the scissors. No trace of my little craft project can be left behind.

I wipe my forehead and saunter out of my office, trying to look nonchalant. Inside, I'm beaming with pride. I've never put myself in such a dangerous position before, but I feel so alive. So confident. I'm ready for the rally.

I screech out of the university parking lot and speed over to Ryan's apartment, pick him up, and tear through downtown. Once parked in the nearest garage, I hightail it down the sidewalk to Westlake Center, almost leaving him in the dust.

My efforts pay off, and Ryan and I arrive before the rally starts. We stake out seats amongst the folding chairs on the plaza. It's a crisp, sunny day in downtown Seattle, perfect for an outdoor event. I'm beginning to think the Senator can even control the weather.

We're sitting right next to the microphone stands in the aisles. I'm counting on them taking questions from the audience at some point during this thing. They have to, otherwise my entire plan is ruined. But judging by the mics they have ready to go, I'm sure they will. And I'm definitely going to take my turn.

51

Thalia

After clearing me for entry, the security guard at Westlake Center holds open the door. With a deep breath and a nod of thanks, I glide through, fidgeting with the buttons on my blouse. My hands are shaking.

It appears my body knows what my mind refuses to accept. I absolutely, positively, should not be at this rally.

Warren doesn't know that I'm here, and he never will. He's at the restaurant as he should be, so he won't even know that I've left the girls with the nanny again. But that doesn't change the fact that I'm lying to him.

Yesterday, I quit this job. I didn't allow myself to have a second thought, because I was afraid I would change my mind. Instead, I flew home like the kids on the last day of school before summer vacation, flung my arms around Warren's neck and sobbed my apologies into his shoulder. I begged his forgiveness, which he granted and sealed with a kiss before dashing out the door to get to the restaurant. I can't say it fixed everything wrong with our relationship, but I felt like I was doing the right thing for the first time in weeks.

As eager as I was to divorce Warren a few weeks ago, his phone call yesterday shook me to my core. Am I really ready to destroy the family we've built? Break Warren's heart? And the children's spirits? Could Harris really be worth all that?

Of course not. I know this.

But I also know that I love him. Don't I? Every thought of him sends a secret shiver through my body, ending in a smile I suppress because it's too private to be shared. I've never once felt that with Warren.

It doesn't matter, though, because I'm not wealthy or beautiful enough to be frivolous. I'm average, and average women have to be rational. Sure, Harris is infatuated with me, but does he love me the same way I love him? He's made me no promises. I could sacrifice my family for Harris, then lose him, too. I'd end up with nothing, and I'd deserve it.

This affair has been exhilarating, but if I'm honest with myself, I always knew it couldn't last.

So yesterday afternoon I said a mental goodbye to Harris, changed back into my yoga pants, and went to work making snacks for the girls.

It didn't even occur to me to block his number on my phone.

He texted me. He asked me to meet him at some fancy hotel I've never even heard of. I admit I was tempted. And I didn't trust myself to resist, so I deleted the text before I could memorize the time and place.

I stayed up half the night thinking about it, anyway.

I wanted to wake up fresh this morning. Today is a new day, after all. But I still can't get Harris off my mind. He seemed so sad when I left him yesterday. Maybe even desperate? I know he's been anxious about this rally today, and I felt so guilty leaving him to brave it all alone.

He just needs a little support. That's the only reason I came here, to check on him.

As soon as I know he is okay, I'll go right home. I'll get there before Warren, and everything will go back the way it was before.

But Harris still needs my help. Just for today.

Now that I'm inside the staging area, I elbow my way through the throng of assistants, searching for Harris. Before I can find him, a hand clamps down on my shoulder and squeezes. I wince under the pressure and turn to look behind me.

It's Senator Cox. His icy blue eyes bore into me and I want to run away. I've seen this man on television for years, but never in person. Intimidating isn't the word. He's terrifying.

"Good afternoon, Mrs. Edwards," he says, releasing his grip on my shoulder. He extends his hand to shake mine. "It's lovely to make your acquaintance after all this time. I've heard so much about you."

"Uh, thank you very much," I say, my hand firmly secured in his powerful squeeze. "It's an honor to meet you, sir."

"My son informs me you've been absolutely indispensable these last few days. This is the most difficult period of a campaign, I'm sure you realize." He smiles at me, but the smile doesn't reach those frozen eyes.

"Yes, it's quite stressful, but Harris is managing wonderfully," I say. "I can't really take any credit." I try to extricate my hand, but his grip tightens. He won't let me go.

"We're all very grateful for your assistance," he says. "And we look forward to much more of the same." A shudder ripples up my spine, but I'm not cold. It's him, the

Senator. He's polite, cordial, and more complimentary than I deserve. Even so, I feel threatened, though I can't explain why.

Still keeping my right hand captive, he pulls me to his side and slides his arm tightly around my shoulder. He breathes into my face, "I know we all covet your presence as a long-term member of my son's team." Nothing about this feels like a question.

"Oh, no sir," I protest, "I'm afraid I can't do that. I have a family—"

"Yes, a family," he interrupts. "A husband? Children?" I nod weakly, desperate for him to let me out of his distressing handshake prison.

"And a sister, I've been told," he says. I nod again, swallowing. Sweat drips from my hairline. This tiny backstage area is stifling.

"If you'll excuse me, sir, I need to get some air," I say.

All at once, he releases my grip, smiles broadly, and says, "Of course, of course. Our deepest thanks for your service."

As I back away from him, massaging my hand, he seizes my forearm. "I know Harris will want to thank you. *In person.*" He squeezes me hard enough to leave fingerprints, then grins and releases me for good this time.

He turns the corner and I sag against the wall, trying to process what just happened. What did he mean about Harris wanting to thank me in person? Does he know Harris asked me to meet him at a hotel? It doesn't matter. I absolutely cannot go. I have to be home for Warren.

52

Cleo

"Aren't they amazing? Let's hear it for Senator William Cox and soon-to-be Congressman Harris Cox!!!"

Her enthusiasm is too much for this stuffy rally, but Amber's energy level never takes a dip.

Why they asked Charity Barbie to act as the moderator, I don't understand. Family connections, I guess. But if I had any lingering doubts about her relationship to Harris, they've been alleviated. I've kept my eye on her every time she's bounced up to the podium, vigilant for the slightest sign of chemistry between the two of them. And I haven't caught so much as a glance, never mind a smile or wink. In fact, Harris was scanning the audience half the time, undoubtedly searching for me.

I've made a point of snuggling up to Ryan throughout this whole boring event, nestling my head on his shoulder. Just cozy enough to make Harris go blind with jealousy. Foolish as hell, but I don't have a slimber of discretion left inside myself. After today, Harris will be the one chasing me.

As soon as the crowd's applause dies down, Amber trills into the microphone, "Now for the moment I know you've all been waiting for..." She giggles. "These esteemed gentlemen have agreed to take a few questions from the audience!"

During her announcement, an aide turns on the microphone in the center aisle. I untwine myself from Ryan's arm and vault out of my seat so hastily that I knock over the folding chair I've been sitting on. I stumble over Ryan's legs, trying to get out of the row of seats, causing me to fall into the aisle, banging my pelvis and scraping my hands on the bricks. The commotion draws the attention of the audience, who gasp at my mishap, but I couldn't care less. I clamber up from the ground, straighten my skirt, and lunge for the microphone.

I'm on a mission.

"Question for Senator Cox," I say, pulling the microphone out of its stand. My eyes blaze into his from across the crowd, signaling strength and resolve. I won't back down and I want him to know it.

He motions to Amber, who hands him the on-stage microphone. I charge ahead with my question.

"It's on a subject dear to—"

"Can we get medical support for this young lady?" interrupts Senator Cox in his deep, buttery-smooth voice. "We're so grateful for your attendance here today, Miss..." His icy grin sends a chill up my spine. "...And for your concern with the direction of this wonderful country we all share. But we couldn't live with ourselves if you had injuries that weren't properly looked after, on our account. Could we, Son?"

Harris's face goes white as recognition flashes across it. He wipes his forehead, grabs a bottle of water from under his chair, and chugs it.

I suddenly realize that what I'm about to do will affect him, too. This is the first time I've made a decision without considering the aftermath on Harris. I can only hope I don't regret this; there's no turning back now. All eyes are on me.

Just as I'm about to speak, a latex-gloved hand closes around my wrist. Instinctively, I yank it away and look over my shoulder. Two men hover behind me, dressed in scrubs. The slim, young one holds the first aid kit while the husky older guy prepares to encase my hand in gauze.

The microphone slips in my sweaty palm, and I almost drop it. When I wipe my hand on my skirt, it makes a dark red stain. It's not sweat, it's blood. And it's left a ghastly smear all over the microphone, too. Only now do I notice that the scrapes on my hand are deep enough to require bandages, but that will have to wait. I didn't make it this far, only to sit it out in a first aid tent.

"My question..." I clear my throat. The energy in the audience pulsates with shock at my tenacity to charge ahead in my bloodied state. "...is on a subject dear to the Senator's heart." I pause for dramatic effect, then pull the microphone right up to my lips. "Crime."

A couple of people snicker in the back row.

I glance at Ryan, who is barely touching the edge of his seat. He's always wound tight, but right now he looks dangerously close to snapping. I don't know whether he wants to protect me or punish me.

On the stage, Senator Cox grits his teeth as his face swells into a red rage. I can see his jaw muscles bulging from here.

The husky medic with the gloves on pulls my right hand away from the microphone. This time I don't stop him. He wipes it with an antiseptic pad and bandages it while I speak.

"Could you tell the audience, please, whether you consider yourself tough on crime?" I ask.

"Of course, Miss," says the Senator, performing a believable impression of someone who has never seen me before. "But that is more of a local issue. Perhaps that would be better addressed through your local mayor or police chief. Next question, please."

The commanding power of his voice spurs a nearby security guard into action. He rushes over to me, causing the medics to back away from their task. The guard puts his hands on my shoulders to steer me down the aisle. But I duck out from under him before he can get a solid grip, clutching the microphone as if my life depended upon it.

It might.

He reaches down and seizes my hand — the one holding the microphone — but I just squeeze tighter. He jerks my arm; I spin and almost fall on the bricks. We tussle, right here in the aisle, him trying to wrestle me to the ground and me wriggling desperately away from him. Finally, he catches my opposite forearm and twists it behind my back. He's strong. Too strong for me. I'm locked in this position now, unable to free myself.

My options have just become extremely limited. I can either give up and allow myself to be escorted off the premises, or I can use the only thing I have left. This microphone.

I have to try. If I don't, the Senator will never allow me to access him again.

"I HAVE," I grunt as the guard twists my arm into my back, "A FOLLOW-UP QUESTION."

Ryan rises to his feet, twitching like he's gearing up for a fight.

The Senator grips the podium, panting through his nose like a bull before he charges.

The guard's clipped voice hisses into my ear. "Let's go." He cements my defeat by spinning me around and death marching me down the aisle.

"STOP."

I know that voice. It penetrates me like a golden sunbeam. A smile spreads across my lips.

He's come to my rescue.

"Release this woman," Harris says. "She's done nothing wrong."

The guard unhands me, but can't resist a slight shove as he does so.

Harris's eyes connect with mine from across the audience. "Please, Miss," he says. "Continue with your follow-up question."

I smile and straighten my shoulders, the gloat bubbling up from inside me.

"Would you, Senator, commit to sponsoring a bill aimed at protecting the victims of the very serious crime of hit-and-run?"

A dull question, to be sure, but I'm just setting the stage.

"You'll need to contact my office if you'd like me to consider sponsoring new legislation." The Senator's voice has gone flat. He points to the audience. "Next, please."

I clear my throat and continue. At least a dozen people are recording this on their phones, and the news cameras have moved in closer. My big moment has arrived. I couldn't have planned it better if I'd tried.

"I once witnessed a terrible accident..." I scan the audience, addressing them directly. "A little girl walked right out in front of a car. She was alone. The driver didn't —" My voice catches. "—see her."

Despite my resolve, this will always be a tender subject. I swallow and go on.

"He ran right over her. She had no chance. She died in minutes, right in front of me."

The atmosphere is electric with anticipation. I can feel the audience hanging on my every word, desperate to know where this story ends up.

"The driver left the scene. He got away with it. But worst of all—"

I reach into my jacket pocket and pull out an envelope.

"A certain powerful individual knows what happened that day. And worked very hard to cover it up. To protect his own interests."

I hold the envelope high in the air, so everyone can see.

"I know who the guilty party is, and I have the proof."

The audience emits a collective gasp.

"I'd like to know that when I take it to the authorities, they will hold the guilty party accountable."

The rally erupts into chaos. Audience members whisper to each other. Cameras snap photos and record video. An elderly gentleman presses himself to his feet and approaches the stage. People in the back boo and hiss. A formidable-looking woman relieves me of the microphone, which I'm all too happy to be rid of now that I've completed my mission. She speaks into it, demanding answers.

The Senator has already motioned to security, who moves in to remove me. Several guards are about to descend, and they won't fail this time.

Ryan stands at his seat, bewildered, no doubt wondering whether he should stay by my side or abandon me to my fate.

And Harris. Harris paces the back of the stage, his head in his hands. He coughs, then coughs again. He doubles over, his hand to his throat. Is he choking?

No one notices him amidst the madness. He coughs some more and repeatedly tries to clear his throat. I scream. "He's choking! Someone help him! Harris is choking!"

I can't be heard above the crowd. Panic overtakes me. I have to get to him.

I push forward, but I'm stopped as four security guards in bulletproof vests surround me. They grab my arms and drag me backwards, away from the stage. Away from Harris.

My eyes never leave Harris as I plead with the guards to help him.

But someone did notice.

A woman appears from backstage and hands him a fresh bottle of water. She rubs his back and whispers in his ear until he calms down.

It's not just any woman.

It's my sister.

Her eyes dart out over the audience, halting when they catch mine. The tumult melts away as we connect, each of us aghast at the sight of the other.

I almost don't notice the security guards grabbing me. They spin me around backwards, breaking my gaze from Thalia.

Flanked by the guards, cameras click as I'm marched down the aisle. Once we've gotten outside the audience seating area, the guards loosen their grip.

"You'll need to leave the rally immediately," says the one with the beard and shaved head. "Or we'll charge you and have you trespassed."

The questions shouting in my head drown his voice out. What the hell is Thalia doing backstage at Harris's event? What secrets is she keeping from me?

"Yes, Sir," I mumble. "Sorry for your trouble."

The female guard with the slicked-tight bun rolls her eyes. She steps between him and me. She'd be an inch from my face if she was tall enough. "Time to go, Ma'am."

That's fine with me. I came here to let the Senator know he can't control me, and I've accomplished that. Ryan is somewhere out there in the crowd, but I can't take the risk of waiting for him one second longer. The last thing I need is to get arrested for trespassing.

Just before I walk away, I remember the one thing I still need to do. It's so important, I can't believe I almost forgot.

The envelope in my hand contains a copy of the receipt from the day of the accident, which is enough to signal that I have hard evidence to connect Senator Cox to the coverup.

I hand it to the bearded guard and tell him to give it to the Senator.

"He'll know what it is," I say.

Then I escape, speed-walking down the street. I'll slip into the parking garage and drive home. Ryan will have to fend for himself.

53

Harris

My father's muffled yell, penetrating the door of this tiny single-stall bathroom, is getting angrier. Ironic that he's not addressing me, but everyone else in the vicinity. If he showed enough respect to speak to me directly, I might even listen.

But he won't, and there's no way I'm coming out until I talk to Cleo.

I wait through several rings until her voicemail picks up. I hang up. Again. It's the fourth time.

I need to talk to her.

"Harris?" comes Iris's voice through the heavy, locked door. "Harris, can you open the door for me? We need you to come out and deal with this."

So Dad has already turned my own assistant against me. I won't dignify this with a response.

Where are you, Cleo?

I call her again and wait through the fruitless ringing. Why did she do this? Why did she show up to this rally, which is so important to my campaign, and sabotage me in front of my father and everyone?

And after I came to her defense.

I limped through this event today as it was. The stress is killing me. I vomited three times before going out there to read that speech. In this very bathroom.

When Cleo's voicemail picks up again, I want to throw my phone across the room. But it's my only link with her right now, and my hand just won't ungrasp it. I bang my phone on my forehead a few times, lean back against the wall, and sink to the floor. It's filthy, but I don't care. I don't deserve better than this right now.

Everything is crashing down around me. Cleo was the only thing I ever really needed. I made one stupid mistake fifteen years ago, and I let my father take her away. I've played games with her, leading her on and letting her down. Using her sister as a substitute. I've let this get out of all control.

I've never been able to stand up to my father. If Cleo exposes what I did… that I killed a child and covered it up… it will be my own fault.

My weakness has turned the one person who always loved me into my most fearsome enemy.

I give up on calling Cleo. She obviously doesn't want to hear from me now.

I hold out a flicker of hope that she'll respond when she sees all my missed calls, even though I know she shouldn't. She's been nothing but loyal to me and I've been nothing but trouble to her.

Outside the bathroom door, I hear Iris talking to my father. She tells him the crowd is dispersing, and the press is requesting a statement on the woman at the microphone and her bizarre tale.

There's no mistaking my father's response: "Harris will give a statement."

With no further coercion, I get to my feet, brush myself off, and exit my bathroom stall shelter. There's no way out of this.

I don't want to win this election anymore. I just want out. But I know that's a false hope. I'm sure now that my father has done far more than I'll ever be aware of to guarantee that I get elected to Congress.

I'm trapped.

So I do what I have to do. Paste on my smile and go find the reporter to make my statement on the stranger at the microphone.

54

Thalia

I had to separate myself from the chaos, so I slipped away to the food court inside. I'm comfortable here. The table is sticky with spilled soda and there's a forgotten kid's meal toy on it. It reminds me of Daisy and Dot.

I miss them. I should be home with them right now.

What am I doing here? This world of power and corruption is not for me. I'm buried in regret, but I'm not ready to dig my way out. Something is holding me down. There's a reason I don't feel I can just walk away.

It's Harris. He might still need me.

At this moment, I don't even know where he is. Maybe he's with Cleo.

She doesn't know that I've been working for Harris. I've been diligent to hide that fact from everyone, mostly so that Warren doesn't find out.

Why didn't it occur to me that Cleo might show up at one of Harris's events? If I'd had the courage to be honest with myself, I would have admitted that she's never stopped loving him. That couldn't be more clear.

She would follow him to the end of the earth. Of course she'd come to a rally.

I can't understand how she caused such a scene that the rally was shut down. Since I was backstage, I missed most of it. Only after I came out to calm Harris did I see her being manhandled by the gang of guards.

What an idiot I am. Now that she's seen me with Harris, she'll know the truth. She'll never forgive me. Their relationship was over years ago, but still. I've betrayed my sister. My flesh and blood.

As soon as I get a chance, I'll call her and explain. I'll tell her how innocent we've been. We haven't done anything other than kiss. We're not much more than… boss and employee. He did hold me in his bed, but that's all. Even Warren wouldn't be too upset if he knew.

Who am I kidding? I don't even believe myself.

Harris finally appears. He emerges from the bathroom and is immediately surrounded by everybody except me. He straightens his tie, but he still looks terrible. His hair is rumpled and his shoulders are slumped.

My heart yearns to comfort him. He needs someone who cares, and right now that someone is me.

I get up from the sticky table and head towards him. Before I get close, the Senator spots me. He breaks away from security and strides in my direction. His cold blue eyes bore into me, making me long to run home to Warren's strong arms and forget this whole thing.

Before I can send the message to my legs, he restrains me with his imposing presence. "Mrs. Edwards," he says. I stop. It's too late to run. "Yes, Sir?"

"It seems you are failing in your duties as my son's assistant."

I swallow. I want to tell him I already quit, but my throat is too dry. When I open my mouth to speak, nothing comes out.

He looms over me. I bite my lip.

"As you are Harris's personal assistant," he says, "with no apparent skills other than babying him, it's time you get back to work doing just that. He needs to get out there and make a statement on camera. Go do whatever it is you do to calm him down and get him to do what's best for himself, and more importantly, his career."

Somehow I squeak out a "yes, sir," and move my leaden feet in Harris's direction. Before I get two steps, Senator Cox has his snaky hand on my shoulder. I turn to see him smiling, the most beguiling smile I've ever seen.

"I'd like you to know, Mrs. Edwards, that you are obviously cut out for this type of work." He squeezes my shoulder ever so lightly. "Caring for a public figure like my son requires a sympathetic, devoted soul, such as yourself. If you'd like to stay on as Harris's assistant permanently, I can make sure you - and your family - are very well taken care of." His grip has firmed, and his pointed suggestion makes it clear a reply is required.

Just as I'm about to refuse, Iris, Harris's real assistant, gets the Senator's attention. "Excuse me, sir, I've got an update for you," she says. The Senator releases me. "We've got a remote team mobilizing now, as you requested."

"And?" he asks. Iris has him distracted for the moment, and I sense this is my opportunity to escape.

As I do, I hear her say, "They're confident they can locate her."

What is it with these people? They're always keeping secrets.

I get another pang of longing for Warren, surprising myself yet again. I'm not sure if I miss him in particular, or just the comfort of home with him and the girls.

That will have to wait, though, because I have a

politician to baby.

Harris is surrounded by a mob, but the sadness in his expression reveals how alone he is. Security, Westlake Center staff, campaign staff, and some people I don't recognize swarm around him. The press would like to join, but they've been relegated to a separate room with their cameras, waiting for Harris to come and make the statement I'm supposed to talk him into giving.

I elbow my way through the miniature mob. Parasites, all of them.

I take Harris's face in my hands and gently direct his eyes toward mine. For a moment, it's like we're the only ones in the world. His eyes look different than usual, though. Defeated. Hopeless.

Compassion overwhelms my heart. This poor man. Is he just being used by everyone around him, including his own father?

"Can you do this?" I ask.

He just shakes his head. No.

"Do you want to?"

He shakes his head again. I sigh.

"Then quit. Drop out. Don't do this if you don't want to," I say.

He lets out the tiniest sarcastic chuckle and shakes his head one more time.

"Come see me tonight," he says. "At the Edgewater."

It's my turn to shake my head. "I can't, Harris. I have to go home."

He grabs my wrists tightly, pulls me close, and says in my ear, "Tonight, Thalia. The Edgewater. For me. Please."

I can't say yes, but I can't say no, either.

"Go make your statement," I say.

We'll see.

55

Cleo

I've found my way to the top of the hill in Gas Works Park again. A cold, wet wind has picked up, punishing me as it whips my face and numbs my lips. But no one will find me here, and I need time to think.

I have mixed feelings about what happened today. I've turned the tables on Senator Cox. Now he knows I won't surrender to him, nor to the goons he sent to menace me. Will he send them back? Maybe. But at least I've shown I'll fight for myself.

And if I was clear at the rally, he should understand that I'm the one with the power now. I possess evidence both to implicate Harris in the accident, and the Senator in the cover-up. They're both in jeopardy if they cross me.

The Senator is dangerous, and I'll have to stay one step ahead to continue outwitting him. But I'm satisfied with the current state of affairs.

What I don't like is putting Harris's future in a precarious position. If Senator Cox forced me to reveal the evidence of the accident, Harris's involvement would be exposed. He was, after all, the driver of the car that killed the girl. The damage to his public image would destroy his career.

I can't let it get that far. Harris means everything to me. He's the reason I'm doing all this. For him… and for us.

He'll understand.

I swipe the raindrops off my hair, and the thoughts out of my head. I didn't climb to the top of the hill to ponder father and son Cox. Not today.

Today, I'm agonized over my sister.

What was Thalia doing at that rally? The question tortures me. I scour my brain for an acceptable explanation for her presence. But there's nothing.

She wasn't just at the rally, taking up an uncharacteristic interest in politics. She was backstage. With Harris. MY HARRIS.

Anger wells up inside me, but I shove it back down.

Thalia is my baby sister. I raised her. What is she keeping from me? I could just call and ask her myself, but I don't want to get blinded by lies. If I can figure out her game before I call, I'll be prepared.

Maybe it wasn't really her. Maybe I'm paranoid because I was so nervous about confronting the Senator.

But I know my own sister.

We made eye contact.

Of course, it was her.

But why?

I suck in a few deep breaths of cool, misty air. The fresh smell of grass and rain clashes with the sour taste in my mouth. I've swallowed my own lie, and it's threatening to come back up.

Harris will never understand.

I told him I would be there for him, tried to support and

encourage him. But then I showed up and sabotaged him in front of everyone. My only concern was getting the Senator off my back. I didn't consider how it would affect Harris at all. My mind was only on one track: get out of trouble. Eliminate the threat.

How foolish to think my plan would get Harris out of trouble, too, by ensuring the accident would stay quiet. The Senator would never bring the accident back into the public eye if there was any chance Harris could be connected to it. Better for it to stay forgotten and in the past.

I thought it would be good for Harris and me. Our shared secret would stay where it belongs, in the history we both share.

But I've put a megawatt spotlight back on the accident. It was nothing but an old memory covered in dust until the spectacle I made this afternoon. If there are any real journalists left in Seattle, they'll go digging for the story.

I've forfeited whatever points I made with the encouraging text I sent Harris this morning. Now I have to find a way to make it up to him.

My thoughts zing back to the evidence I stashed in my office. The Senator is probably hunting for it as we speak. That hollow book and its contents are the most precious possessions I have at the moment, and I have no way to protect them. I hate having them out of my sight.

As far as I can tell, I haven't been followed to the park. I'm tempted to retrieve the book out of my office and take it home with me. I could sleep with it by my bed. Or even in my bed.

But if someone broke in to my place during the night, there's no way I could prevent them from taking it.

I decide to leave it in my office and pray the Senator doesn't track it down by some sick magic.

56

Harris

Here I am again, alone in this stupid room in the Edgewater Hotel, waiting for a woman who will not come.

Decidedly drunk.

I've been leaning against the wall draining shot after shot, waiting for Thalia. I knew she wouldn't come. But I waited just the same. Because Dad told me to.

He made me promise — again — that I would get the tape with Thalia tonight. After my breakdown this afternoon, I'm pretty sure she'll never come back.

Even if her judgment was pathetic enough to meet me here, I wouldn't be able to perform anyway. I don't have it in me to lure her into bed. Especially under false pretenses. She's a lovely, honorable woman who doesn't deserve to be involved in all this. My father's deceptions have finally gone too far, even for me.

I can't do any of this.

I'm not my father. I don't even want to be anymore. I just want out.

What could I use? The bourbon glass in my hand? I

don't think you can drink yourself to death in one sitting.

My anti-anxiety meds are on the bureau, but they're nowhere near enough to end me.

People hang themselves in hotel rooms, don't they? Vague images of neckties holding slumping bodies tied to doorknobs comes to mind.

But I don't know how to hang myself. The last thing I want to do is *half*-hang myself.

I wander over to the open window. This room is on the top floor. I could jump off the balcony.

But I don't have the guts.

Nor do I want to spill my guts all over the Seattle sidewalk.

It doesn't matter; there's no sidewalk down there, anyway. Just the Puget Sound.

Maybe I should go drown in it.

Or maybe I'm just wallowing in self-pity.

I'll be fine. As soon as Cleo gets here.

No, Thalia.

As soon as Thalia gets here.

Day Before Election Day

57

Cleo

The gray light drifting through my window wakes me from a restless night. I vault out of bed, shower, and grab some coffee to go. I should be exhausted after yesterday, but there's still so much to do before the election tomorrow.

More than anything, I want to go to my office and make sure my evidence is still intact, but I can't. If I'm being surveilled, I can't do anything so out of the ordinary as show up to the office this early. If there were anywhere else to store it, I would, but I have no secure location. I've reconsidered the safe deposit box idea, but I don't kid myself that the Senator couldn't get into it somehow if he pulled the right strings.

So until I come up with a better plan, the office it is.

The most important task of the day is to make things right with Harris. Tomorrow is the big day, and I want to be there for him when he wins. Be *with* him when he wins.

I've dreamed of tomorrow night for months now, and I can't let yesterday's theatrics change that. He'll be busy all day, and he might even think he doesn't have time to see me. But that's never stopped me before.

Harris wants me, and only me. Deep down, I know he does. Whoever that other woman was has become irrelevant. She can't affect me anymore. I know Harris will be as happy with me as I will be with him.

The one last thing I have to figure out is Thalia. I need to know what she was doing backstage at Harris's rally. The thought of her handing him that bottle of water and whispering in his ear makes me nauseous. But I push that sick feeling back down, as I've been doing diligently since yesterday afternoon.

There has to be a good explanation.

So. Plan for the day: Head over to Thalia's house to talk with her before she gets the girls off to school. She'd never expect a visit from me at this hour. With the element of surprise on my side, she just might tell me the truth.

After that, I'll head to my office, check on my evidence, and appear at my ten o'clock class. I've already scheduled a T.A. to take my afternoon class, so I can track down Harris and meet him tonight.

I'll confess to my terrible judgment and beg for his forgiveness. He'll understand that I confronted his father at the rally for us, so we could put this whole accident behind us forever.

And then we can kiss and make up.

He'll forget all about the other woman. I already have.

And we'll be together tomorrow night at his victory party.

58

Thalia

"Can I make you some coffee?" I ask. Cleo's never been to my house so early in the morning before, and she has never come here unannounced.

The way she looks at me makes me squirm. I don't want a confrontation, but it may be impossible to avoid.

"No, thanks," she says. I serve her some anyway. I make the best coffee in Ballard.

"So what's up?" I ask. "This is pretty early for you to visit."

She shifts in her chair and plays with her coffee without drinking it. Then she looks up at me with a shine in her eyes I haven't seen in years. She definitely has an ulterior motive.

"How much attention have you been paying to Harris's campaign?" she asks. It's my turn to shift in my chair. She knows I'm working for Harris.

I haven't told anyone. Not Warren, not the girls. I've been extremely vigilant to keep it a secret, but that ceased to matter when Cleo saw me onstage with him.

"Some..." I say.

"So you know about the rally yesterday." It's not a question. Her gaze burns me up. I can't sit here and lie to her face. I get up and move to empty the dishwasher.

"I do," I say.

"You were there."

I put some glasses in the cabinet. "Yes." I hate this.

"Why?"

Silverware clanking into the drawer now. I can't look at her, and I can't lie. "I care about him. Uh, his campaign."

She pushes up from her chair. Her hands slam a little too hard on the table, making coffee jump out of her mug. "Why were you backstage, Thalia?"

I freeze, butcher knife in mid-air, its journey to the knife drawer halted for the moment. The air chokes on her question, but I can't answer. As far as Cleo knows, the last time I saw Harris was at the family dinner with him weeks ago.

"Why. Were. You. Backstage," she repeats.

I swallow. "I'm sorry, Cleo. It's time for the girls to go to school. We'll have to talk about this later," I say. "Daisy! Dot! Time to go!"

The girls come running out of their bedroom, backpacks flying. "Auntie Cleo!" they holler on their way to the garage. Children can be an excellent distraction.

"Thalia," she says again. This time, she grabs my wrist. "Answer me." She's caught me, like a fish on a hook. There is no good way to answer her. I can't let her know what has been going on between Harris and me. I just can't.

I inhale and press my lips together.

Her phone rings in her handbag. The shock of it releases her grip on my wrist just enough for me to pull it away.

"I have to get the girls to school, Cleo. We'll talk later."

59

Cleo

Thalia practically pushed me out the door the second my phone rang. The caller ID let me know it was Ryan, so I ignored it.

No doubt he's furious with me. After inviting him to accompany me to the rally, I caused a disturbance of epic proportions, then abandoned him to his own devices. The press was rabid, and it's possible they're hounding him since they can't get a hold of me.

Is that my fault? He's a grown man; he can handle it.

I slide into my car, fire it up, and take my place in the morning commute. On the way to the university, my mind scrutinizes every aspect of my brief interaction with Thalia. She admitted to nothing, but her extreme commitment to avoidance is an admission in itself.

She's hiding something big. A secret. But she won't confess to me, so how am I supposed to uncover it?

My thumbs tap the steering wheel, impatient. I'm desperate to get to my office, to check on my book safe.

It will be exactly as I left it. It has to be.

My phone beeps, notifying me I've received a voicemail. I tap, wait, enter my pin, wait.

Ryan's voice spills from the phone. Not angry, though. Panicked.

"Cleo… It's back… the SUV… the guys with the guns… I don't know what you're into, but this is seriously jacked up…"

Oh, no.

Has the Senator dispatched his minions to Ryan's place?

My stomach drops. This is my fault. I involved Ryan in this in the first place, by framing him for the envelope I left at Harris's campaign office. And just when it seemed like the Senator's people had left him alone, I brought Ryan back into it by using him to make Harris jealous at the rally. God, I'm a terrible person.

I call Ryan, preparing to offer a sincere apology and a promise to get rid of the black SUV guys, even if I don't know how.

He doesn't pick up.

I glance at the clock on my dashboard. Can I make it to my ten o'clock class if I stop by Ryan's apartment first? It's doubtful, but I'm foolish enough to try. Running in to check on him will only take a few minutes, and it's the least I can do.

I leave him a message saying I'm on my way over.

I will fix everything today.

And by tonight, all will be right with my world.

60

Harris

My head is pounding. Should I have gone through with the whole killing myself thing last night? It would have gotten me out of my obligations for today. So maybe I should have. But I utterly lack the courage.

Besides, it's too late now.

I open the curtains and the light blinds me. I can't do this. There's no way I can stomach any last-minute door-knocking, begging for votes. I'm sick of everything. All the lies. The deception. The hiding. For what? So I can be like my father. The closer I get to that, the more repulsed I am by the concept.

I'll stay in the hotel all day. Order room service and wallow in self-pity. Hide from the public and pretend none of this is happening.

My cell phone rings. Damn it, did I leave that thing on? It's Iris. I don't have the heart to ignore her. She's been nothing but loyal to me.

She wants to know where I am. And why I'm not at the office. We were supposed to have a meeting this morning,

I guess? I don't know my schedule.

"I can't make it," I say. No further explanation. "You can do whatever you want with the staff for the day. I'm unreachable." I hang up before she can object.

Just as I'm about to turn the phone off, it rings again. Cleo this time. Against my better judgment, I answer. I won't talk about what happened yesterday at the rally. I don't know what she's trying to do, but I want no part of it.

"Harris." She sighs my name, like a goddess.

My inner boundary dissolves. I'm hers.

"I have to see you," she breathes. "To wish you luck for tomorrow."

I don't want luck, but suddenly there's nothing I want more than Cleo's presence.

"Yes. Come to the Edgewater this afternoon." I'll try to clean up my pathetic self before she arrives.

A click on the phone lets me know another call is coming in. My father, no doubt. I don't answer.

I give Cleo my room number, hang up, turn my phone off, and collapse on the bed. Finally, no one can reach me unless they show up in person. A few cleansing breaths gives me the strength to push myself up and stumble to the bathroom.

I turn on the shower, and the room phone rings. I forgot about that. Damn it.

I know who it is. Unless I flee the country, he will find me. I sigh and answer.

"Hi, Dad."

He tells me I'd better get that sex tape with Thalia tonight. It's crucial.

"Cleo is off the rails," he says, "and you know it."

I don't like where this is going.

"She can't be controlled, and she will destroy you if we allow it. I've had to put into place some rather unpleasant precautions, but even that won't be enough. We need the tape. Tonight. No questions asked."

I pull at my hair. "Yes, Dad," I say. I have no fight left.

"And one more thing, Son. You are not to leave that hotel room under any circumstances today. I can tell you are in no shape to be seen by the public. We'll have to cover for you."

"That won't be a problem." I had no intention of leaving, anyway.

"You let me take care of the next twenty-four hours," he says. "I've already delayed my flight until Tuesday night."

61

Cleo

Ryan hasn't called me back, and I've tried his number three more times since I decided to swing by his apartment. A dark storm of foreboding gathers in my head. Something is wrong.

I listen to his voicemail again as I pull up to his building. His voice falters and shakes. This is not a joke or a plea for attention. Ryan is terror stricken.

If the men in the black SUV really are there to pay him a visit, he is right to be.

My breathing quickens as I grasp how stupid I'm being. If Ryan is in mortal danger, I'm about to walk right into it. But this is all my fault.

Ryan has nothing to do with the Senator's vendetta against me.

I clamber out of my car, speedwalk up the steps to the building door, and yank the handle. In my frantic state, I forgot it would be locked. I stumble backwards, catching myself before I fall down the stairs. Anxiety blurs my eyes, but I search and find his name on the doorplate to buzz him.

I chew my thumbnail as I wait.

But there's no answer.

I buzz again.

Still no answer.

What do I do now?

I'll follow someone else into the building. Lots of people should be coming and going at this time of the morning. I crane my neck around the corner to get a view of the parking garage.

The gate opens, and a vehicle exits.

A black SUV.

I dive behind a tall bush to avoid being seen. Between the leaves, I strain to get a glimpse of the driver as he passes.

There's no mistaking him.

It's Savedra.

With his partner in the passenger seat.

What have they done? Tied Ryan up? Knocked him out?

I have to get to him now.

A woman with a baby stroller comes out of the building and I slip in behind her before the door closes.

I bound up the stairs, not willing to wait for the elevator. When I find his door, I pound on it.

My heart hammers in my chest and my breathing is ragged. Sweat rolls down my forehead.

I pound on the door again. "Ryan? Ryan!"

Nothing. No response.

I jiggle the knob, but it's locked. Our relationship never reached the point of exchanging keys, so I have no way in.

What should I do? Alert building management? Call the police? Call Harris?

I can't call Harris, for so many reasons, even though he

may be the only one who could call off the Senator's dogs.

I'll call the police. I should have called them the day Savedra and Forester broke into my place.

No. I should have called them the day of the accident before I let Harris drive me away.

Better late than never to do the right thing.

I call and wait, pacing the hallway and trying Ryan's phone over and over.

Twenty minutes later, an officer arrives for a welfare check. After a few attempts to reach Ryan, he breaks open the door. I try to follow him inside the apartment, but he won't allow it.

I pace again, my mind furiously reviewing the possibilities. Is Ryan alive in there? Is he even home? I pray this was a misunderstanding; that I'll see Ryan in my office again and laugh about this.

The officer emerges from the apartment, speaking into his radio. He doesn't glance my way.

He's left the apartment door ajar. One glimpse of the officer tells me he's oblivious to my presence. He's forgotten I'm here.

I grab the opportunity to peek inside.

A gasp overtakes me and my hand claps over my mouth. Ryan's body is slumped on his couch, surrounded by a vast quantity of bright red blood. I jerk my head back outside, almost involuntarily. The pooling blood reminds me far too much of the little girl's blood spreading on the dirt road as I held her in my lap.

I didn't kill either of them myself, but I still feel responsible.

Something burns inside me. A need to see Ryan. To force myself to look at what I've done. To punish myself? Maybe.

The officer is still talking on his radio. I take advantage of his distraction to sneak into Ryan's apartment. I stand in front of Ryan. Force myself to look at him. The hole in his head and the gun in his hand.

He didn't do this.

There's a note. In front of him on the coffee table, close enough to have his blood spattered on it. A single sheet of white paper with a message printed in black marker, big and bold.

I snatch my phone out of my handbag and take a photo of the note before I ease back through the door. The officer is none the wiser, and I escape down the stairs before he notices me.

Once in my car, I click on the photo and study the note. Is it Ryan's handwriting? I don't know. He's never had an occasion to write anything for me. But whomever wrote this note obviously meant for it to be found.

The message is brief, but strange. Reckless, erratic. It reads:

i know you can never be my GIrlfriend
eVEry minUte we're aParT Hurts mE
thE pain of liVIng is worse than D Eath
i am Not a good matCh for you, dEar CLEO
i hOpe you'Re willing to be mY lOve
in the next life
circUmstAnces aRE agaiNst us
but i must EXpress my devoTion to you
i mean every word

I stare at the note for a few minutes. This message is meant for me. It's addressed to me directly.

Ryan didn't kill himself. He still thought there was a chance for us. He would have fought for me, not just ended his life like this.

I have to figure out what this note means. Fast.

62

Harris

Two plates of raspberry pancakes, half a pot of coffee, and enough smoked salmon to satisfy all the feral cats in Seattle are not enough to bury the question that torments me.

Am I really going to do this?

I stare out the window of this beautiful hotel room, so tidy, swept clean of all previous transgressions that may have been committed here, pondering whether I'm about to commit the most heinous of them all.

And I know the answer is yes. I am going to do this.

I don't care about anything anymore. My life has gotten so out of control that I realize, almost from outside myself, that I've stopped trying. If my father wants to control my every move, I might as well let him. It's so much easier than fighting him, knowing he always wins in the end.

So when he ordered me to get Thalia to the hotel room tonight, I called her. I told her a lie.

Well, only half a lie. My father has taught me well.

I said I needed her for one last thing. If she would come

by my room tonight, I said I'd tell her about it. And then, after that, she could be done. Go back to her husband and children.

So she's on her way here.

I'm really going to do this.

I've forgotten how to care.

63

Cleo

It's been a hell of a day. Finding Ryan dead in his apartment has shaken my resolve.

I weaved in and out of traffic all the way to work, obsessing about the note the whole way. Without the ability to examine it, I couldn't figure out what it meant. But I had plenty of time to consider the possibility of Ryan killing himself. And whether he could have been murdered. If he was, who could have done it? There is one obvious suspect.

But I didn't let this horrific drama sidetrack me from my first priority. Harris. He will always matter the most.

I narrowly missed sideswiping a motorcyclist when I stupidly changed lanes at the same time as I scrolled through my contacts to find Harris's number. Nevertheless, I called, we talked, and I invited myself to his hotel room. He accepted, but first I had to fulfill my work obligations.

I made it to the university without a minute to spare. No time to stop by my office and check on the security of the evidence I have stashed inside.

After delivering a distracted lecture, I dismissed class early and bolted across campus. Sweating, I reached my building and raced up the stairs. My door looked untouched. No sign of forced entry. But the Senator's people are crafty, so I held my breath as I unlocked the door and went inside.

The room was pristine. No one had been there. I checked my book safe, and it was exactly as I had left it. The relief flooded me so completely I sagged into my desk chair and cried.

I didn't indulge the tears for long. Too many important things to do.

Like figure out the meaning behind the note in Ryan's apartment. It didn't take much brain power to figure out the code. Once I put together all the capital letters and excluded all the lowercase ones, I saw it.

The message is intended for me, all right. It says:

"GIVE UP THE EVIDENCE CLEO OR YOU ARE NEXT"

Senator Cox had Ryan killed as a warning to me.

Surrender my evidence or die? I don't accept this ultimatum. I will survive, and I will keep what is mine. I will protect myself.

And Harris. Somehow, I'll protect him, too. From his father, his own flesh and blood.

Now that I know the extremes to which the Senator will go, I'm desperate to see Harris. Ryan is dead. I know the Senator is behind it. He'd never do the dirty work himself, of course, but I saw his man in black driving away from Ryan's apartment before I went in. This is the second literal casualty of my relationship with Harris. I need to talk to him now.

I call his cell phone, but it goes straight to voicemail. I text, but there's no response. A chill runs through me as I consider… could Harris be dead, too? No. The Senator would never eliminate his legacy like that. But still, I'm desperate to confirm that Harris is alive and well. I assume he's still at the Edgewater, as he said he would be.

I'm in my car and off like a shot. To reach Harris as fast as I can. Nothing will stop me from getting to him now.

64

Cleo

My heart pounds from both exertion and fear. I ran straight to Harris's room without bothering to call or text him again. Will he be inside?

I rap on the door, then put my ear up to it. A faint rustling sound comes from the room, followed by footsteps. I breathe a sigh of relief and stand back. He's here.

But he doesn't answer the door. I rap again. More footsteps, and I think I hear him swear.

An eternity later, the lock clicks. The door opens no more than a crack, and Harris's bloodshot eye appears from behind it.

"Cleo," he says. He doesn't invite me in. He doesn't even open the door wide enough to allow me to see him. But the helplessness in his eye is enough. I'm spurred into action to save this man I love from the destruction we are both headed for.

"You look like you need me," I say. "Lucky for us both, I'm here." Before he can argue, I push the door open. His hair is mussed; he's wearing unzipped pants and no shirt. Before he can object, I take his wrist, spin him around, and push him up against the door, which closes with a quiet thud.

I lean in to kiss him, but he doesn't reciprocate. He stares over my shoulder with a stricken look.

Something's wrong.

Instinctively, I turn around to see what Harris is looking at.

And suddenly, everything descends into slow motion. It's like my brain absorbs one fact at a time, as if that's all it can handle, until the meaning is unmistakable.

The bed is not empty.

There is a woman in it.

She's naked.

She has a mess of curly, dark hair.

She looks like Thalia.

She is Thalia.

Thalia is sleeping with Harris.

MY HARRIS.

MY SISTER IS SLEEPING WITH MY HARRIS.

For one frozen moment, my eyes lock with Thalia's.

Then, as if moving through water, I turn to look at Harris. The moment I meet his gaze, the spell is broken. Fury erupts out of me like a boiling volcano. I have never known this rage before.

I scream, "YOU TRAITOR!" beating Harris's bare chest with my fists. "HOW COULD YOU!" He grabs my wrists, still strong despite the defeated look in his eye.

"NO!" I scream again, fighting against his grip. "MY OWN SISTER! MY FLESH AND BLOOD!"

Harris pulls me tight against his chest, still damp from the sweat shared with my treasonous sibling.

I'm sobbing now, repulsed by the idea of Harris and Thalia sharing a bed, but still seeking comfort from the man I've never been able to stop loving.

In the background, Thalia throws her clothes on and says, "I'm leaving." Harris doesn't respond. By the time she's dressed, my sobs have died down. She slips past me and Harris, out the door without a word. I can't bear to look at her.

Harris and I are alone in the room, but I can't bear to look at him either.

I push him away and walk toward the window, gazing out on the Sound, glittering at night with the reflections from the city.

I have lost everything. The two people I've always loved have conspired to betray me. I've gotten mixed up in some political intrigue plot straight out of an overwrought television movie, which got my boyfriend killed. And my own life is still in danger. I have no idea what Senator Cox is planning for me.

My last trickle of confidence drains away. What do I have left to live for? My job?

For a moment, I ponder going out on the balcony and jumping off into the icy waters of the bay.

But that's not me.

I take a few deep breaths, gather my courage like a storm, and turn to face Harris.

"I will prevail," I say, slowly and carefully.

I mean every word.

And with the most dignity I've ever mustered, I stride past Harris, out of the room, out of the hotel, and out into the night.

65

Cleo

The chill wind coming off of Elliott Bay cuts through me, echoing my mood. Knives slice through my mind, slashing all the memories, the motives, the *people* who have caused me so much agony. I couldn't bring myself to go home after what I saw in Harris's room. My own sister, my blood, betrayed me. Interfered with the only other relationship I've ever valued. Why? Does she want to destroy me?

And Harris. My beloved Harris. Why would he betray me like that?

I stalked out of the Edgewater, exerting supernatural-level control over my emotions, turned left, walked down the waterfront, and screamed. Punching the air, raging, screaming, until I purged everything. Then collected myself again, ready to make a plan. *I will prevail*, I had said to Harris. And I will.

I've meandered my way to the Olympic Sculpture Park, taking solace under an abstract orange eagle. No one will find me here, blending into the dark with the random couple on a first date, or the homeless man with his dog. I vow to myself that I won't go home until I make a plan. This has all gone so wrong.

When I deposited that threatening envelope on Harris's doorstep, I didn't mean for everything to get so out of control. He rejected me; I was angry and hurt, and I wanted to punish him. Stupid, stupid decision. It got Ryan killed and put my life in mortal danger. I can't afford to be so rash.

Where do I find myself now? Thalia has somehow gotten into bed with Harris, the only man I've ever loved, despite the fact that she's married. Harris is in love with me, but can't be with me because his father has forbidden it. Senator Cox is so paranoid about Harris's political future that he has already killed Ryan to protect it. This all started as a mistake that Harris and I made, but Harris's father and my sister have now been compelled into playing this twisted game. How Thalia got sucked in, I don't know, but I'd be willing to bet that the Senator was involved in that, too.

The only way to solve this is to bring it back to what it always was: a problem between Harris and I. I've got to extract all the extraneous characters from this complicated drama.

I lean forward against the cold metal railing, close my eyes, stretch my face out to the sea, and let the cold salty wind cleanse me of all the evil I've ever committed.

I'm sorry. I'm so sorry for all of it.

There are too many things I can never make right. For the first time, I allow myself to think about Ryan. Hot tears trickle, then flow, and finally gush into sobs as I realize what I've done. I wronged him deeply, and now he's paid the ultimate price. I can never bring him back to life. If only I could go back, I wouldn't have dared to provoke the Senator so publicly at the rally. Had I known what a horror I would create, I would never have delivered that stupid envelope to Harris's office.

Worst of all, I can never give that family back their little girl.

The regret overpowers me. I double over, hands on my knees, heaving with sobs and nausea, trying to get a hold of myself.

My phone rings.

I want it to shut up.

There is no one I can talk to. No one to trust.

A shudder of air escapes my lungs as I struggle to catch my breath.

The ringing stops.

For a split second, I'm relieved. But I'm desperate to know… who was it? The caller ID is blocked. What if it was Harris? What if he wants to explain himself? Beg my forgiveness?

The phone rings again.

I fumble to answer. "Hello?" I choke out.

"Good evening, Ms. Tait," responds a resonant, powerful voice.

Oh, no. My stomach lurches. The last person I need to hear from right now.

"Senator."

"I want to extend my deepest condolences for your loss," he says. "I understand you and this gentleman, Ryan, were very close."

The way he purrs Ryan's name makes my blood curdle. "He was just a student," I say.

"Yes, well, some of our acquaintances make a bigger impression on our lives than others, don't you agree?"

"Yes…" I say. I don't know what he's getting at, but I

know he's getting at something.

"I'm certain you'll never forget this young man," he says, slowly and carefully. "Suicide is such a shame, isn't it?"

"Yes," I say again.

"It could happen to any one of us." His words feel pointed, like darts aimed directly between my eyes. "Even you."

His message is received, loud and clear. He had Ryan killed and made to look like a suicide, as a warning to me. But what I don't understand is why. If he knew I was the real threat to Harris's career, why bother with Ryan? Why not just kill me instead? I decide to play along and see if I can get any answers. I know I'm playing with fire, but I'm already in so deep I have nothing left to lose.

"We're all vulnerable, Senator," I say. "But I don't have the slightest clue what would make you think I would ever give up like that. It's not in my nature. But then you know that already." I pause, and he doesn't fill the silence. Still my move. "My turn to pose a question to you. If you can spare a moment of your valuable time. It is election eve, after all."

"Please," he says without emotion. I can feel his curiosity pulsing through the phone lines. He wants desperately to know what I'm up to. This is exactly where I want him.

"As an older, wiser man of the world, don't you ever question these things? For example, I'm wondering why it is that I'm still alive, and Ryan is dead. I'm absolutely certain—" my words are the darts this time "—that you can provide the answer. Why am I still alive?"

He clears his throat, something I've never heard him do. He's stalling for time. Triumph is within reach. I've almost got him bested. But I haven't won this battle yet. I can't let down my guard.

He bursts out with his trademark hearty laugh, the one I've heard on television countless times in interviews and on campaign commercials. It's the laugh that makes men feel like they could share a beer together and makes women feel like he will take care of them. It's the laugh that seems so genuine, but is anything but. Regardless of how phony it is, the glowing liquid warmth of it travels right through the phone into my heart, dispelling the tension. The man is a professional.

"Maybe it's because you made such a public spectacle of yourself yesterday. Or maybe it's because you have something I want." I assume he means the dress and receipts. "Or maybe it's because my fool of a son still loves you."

That last sentence warms me all over again. Despite the sickening scene I witnessed only a short time ago, I know he's right. Whatever was going on with Thalia in that hotel room, I know Harris does love me. We are meant to be together. Despite his psychopath of a father.

"Or maybe I'm just too strong," I say. "Maybe you've underestimated me for years."

He laughs again. "Don't forget. Deaths like Ryan's can be contagious. It would be tragic if it happened to someone else that you loved. Your sister Thalia, for example."

And the line goes dead.

So that's why he called. To threaten me. If I don't back off, he'll come after Thalia. I contemplate this possibility. The longer I think about it, the angrier I get. How dare he tell me what to do? He's controlled my life indirectly for fifteen years, and it's brought nothing but death, destruction, and heartache. And now he's threatening to harm Thalia, even *kill* her? I might be furious with her, but damn if she isn't *my* flesh and blood. I won't let some pompous, arrogant politician bring any harm to her.

This ends tonight. I will bring the curtain down on this horror show if it's the last thing I do on earth. The devastation of that accident cannot keep spiraling into the future, destroying more and more lives forever. I will end this corruption single-handedly if I have to.

I will prevail.

Now the question remains: How? What defense have I against the Senator's formidable powers? I don't even know how deep his powers go. Not to mention how sick and evil his intentions can be. Where do I begin? Everything I've done so far seems amateur at best. Now that he's brought murder into the game, the stakes have gotten to the level of survival, for both me and my loved ones, few though they may be.

What if I just take the information I have about the accident and go public with it? First thing tomorrow morning I could get it all over the news, before the vote. No, that would be stupid. It's too late, anyway. The only thing it would accomplish would be to incriminate Harris and destroy any chance I still might have with him.

I know what I need to do, and where I need to do it.

They'll never agree to come. But I have to try.

Election Day

66

Thalia

The first light of dawn comes up over the horizon. I haven't slept all night. In fact, I never even went home last night. After Cleo caught me in bed with Harris at the Edgewater, I couldn't bear to face Warren. I didn't even call or text him. He's probably going crazy wondering where I am.

I'm sitting in my car a block away from Cleo's condo, mustering up my courage.

I cheated on Warren last night. Harris and I went through with it. Why did I sleep with him? I shouldn't even have shown up at the hotel. But damn it, Warren practically drove me to do it. He lit into me again about being gone all afternoon. All I wanted was to take a little job for a few weeks, to get out of the house and have some time away from the kids. But he wouldn't let me have that without constantly questioning me and nagging me.

That's not true.

I took the job to be closer to a man I admired because I was attracted to his power, charisma, and charm. I was never honest with Warren about where I was going or what I was doing. It was easy to take advantage of the fact that he was working so hard at the restaurant he wouldn't even notice what I was up to. As long as I had someone to watch the girls, he would never be the wiser.

I guess I felt so guilty already that when Warren blew up at me yesterday, I left him out of spite. I stormed out of the house in a huff, leaving the girls and him, and drove straight to Harris's hotel room. Warren had no way to know where I went or whether I would come back, and I didn't care.

I flew down to the Edgewater and right into what I thought would be Harris's welcoming arms. But when I got to his room, he looked sick. Like death was on his mind. Like the end of the world had arrived. The charming smile and the glint in the eye were gone. I'd just left my husband only to find the alternative a shell of his former self. I felt so desperate and crazy that I threw myself at him, hoping to revive the strong, confident man I thought Harris was. We made love without a second thought.

Until Cleo came to the door. Then I had plenty of time to think.

I couldn't face her. I threw on my clothes and ran away before she could say a word to me. The rest of the night I drove all over the city, stopping once for a twenty-ounce mocha at a drive-through bikini barista, and again to splurge on a steak omelet at the 5-Point Cafe. Even the stuffed moose head on the wall looked disappointed in me.

I should feel like a fool. My dalliance with Harris has destroyed everything I cherish. It's messed up my marriage even worse than it already was, coerced me to abandon the girls, compromised my morals with a soon-to-be U.S. Congressman, and ruined my relationship with my sister beyond repair.

If there's one thing I know, it's that Cleo has never given up on Harris. She's loved him forever, and still does. Maybe a part of me wanted to get one over on her. Stick it to her. Be better than her at something besides housewifing. Steal a man from her.

Now I've done it. I should regret it.

But every minute with Harris has been worth it. I've discovered an excitement I didn't know was possible, and I'm not ready to give it up.

I still can't bear to lose Cleo. My sister, my family, the mother figure who was there for me when no one else was. So even though my betrayal doesn't deserve forgiveness, I find myself in desperate need of it, anyway.

I drag myself out of my car, down the block to Cleo's building, and to her door.

I take a deep breath and raise my fist to knock, but I can't.

She has good reason to hate me, and I don't want to see the pain in her eyes. Not only have I stolen something precious from her, I don't intend to give it back. Harris is mine now. We sealed our passion in the hotel room last night. I will secure his commitment in the hotel ballroom tonight.

No, Cleo can wait. Time will heal her wounds.

I have a party to dress for.

67

Harris

Why am I still alive?

This is the first thought that enters my mind when my eyes open this morning. Apparently, I lack the courage to kill myself, but I had hoped that maybe I'd just die in my sleep.

Why am I awake so early?

The sun has barely risen, and I most definitely did not set an alarm last night. After both Cleo and Thalia ran out on me, I sat and contemplated my abominable track record with the Tait sisters. I drank myself into a stupor, curled up on the floor, and passed out.

Before I can bother to answer these trivial questions, the room phone rings. It's so loud. It hurts my head. Somebody make it stop. Me. I'm the only one who can make it stop.

I pick up the receiver.

"Hello," I grunt.

"This is the third time I've called. Where have you been?" my father demands.

"Here," I say. How could he have called twice before? I would have heard it. Wouldn't I? I must have been dead to the world.

"Regardless, I have a car scheduled to come pick you up in fifteen minutes. Be ready when it arrives."

"I'm not going," I say. I can't fathom the idea of leaving this room today. Much less in fifteen minutes.

"Yes, you are," says my father the Senator. This is how he sounds when he expects everyone to obey him. "It's election day and you will follow through on expectations. You now have fourteen minutes."

He's so certain I won't argue that he hangs up on me.

I sit for a minute with the phone in my hand, wondering what to do. I call him back.

"I believe you're down to thirteen minutes," he says upon answering.

"I think," I say, holding my head, "I'll spend the next thirteen minutes my way. Three minutes to pour and drink another bourbon. Two minutes to text Cleo and beg her to forgive me for sleeping with her sister. One minute to smash the SD card with the recording. Then five minutes to bury my head in a pillow to see if I can quit breathing. And when that doesn't work, four minutes to run the bath water, get in and slit my wrists. Is that thirteen? No? I might be down to twelve now. I'd better get to pouring that bourbon."

"Good, you got the tape," he says, unbelievably. "Hand it to the driver I'm sending over. He'll get it to me directly."

Something inside me breaks. The way he disregarded everything I said, in favor of fulfilling his own twisted agenda. All of a sudden, the pattern of his selfishness and manipulation clears through the fog in my mind. How have I missed this? It's as if I've been under his spell my entire life, the same way the public has. He's fooled me into respecting him, when I should have reviled him. I should have separated myself from him, gotten as far away as I could have, years ago.

A rage I've never known detonates inside me like a grenade.

"Of course I got the damn tape!" I yell, not caring who else I disturb in the hotel. "But there's no way in hell you are ever going to get your hands on it. Do you hear me? Ever. I loved Thalia, in whatever way I'm capable of loving, and I used her because you told me to. She hates me now, and with good reason. I deserve whatever I get, but she doesn't!"

"Harris, keep your voice down," he hisses. He never calls me by my name.

But I'm just getting started.

"I love Cleo, too," I say. He needs to hear this as much as I need to say it. "But she caught me with her sister, and she'll never, ever marry me now."

"Marry you?" He actually laughs. "You're forbidden from being with her, you know that. That's been against the rules since — what is it — two thousand three?"

The way he talks to me, as if I'm a child. As if he can still order me around with no regard for my feelings or desires. For the first time, I can see he is sick, maybe even evil. Whatever broke in me is about to be put back together, stronger. I will never acquiesce to him again.

"No," I say. I'm shaking, but I force my voice to come through the phone line calm, confident. "I love Cleo. I always have. All I've ever wanted was to have a life with her. I've let you get so twisted up between us I may have destroyed any chance of that happening. But I will not allow you to continue."

"Son, you're blathering now. Have you had something

to drink already this morning? That driver's almost to the hotel. Why don't you just stay in your room until he arrives? I'll have him deliver you straight to me. We'll sober you up and get this worked out."

As he talks, I dress myself and locate my keys and wallet. I don't know where I'm going, but I can't stay here.

"You should know I don't want to be a congressman, either," I say. This is true, but I'm mostly saying it to hurt him. To create a crisis in his matrix of control. The polls have swung dramatically in my favor the last few days, and I have a strong feeling that my father has pulled some significant — probably illegal — strings. I will win today, no matter what I do. "I don't care in the slightest what happens. You can text me the results tonight."

I hang up on him this time, leaving him in what I can only hope is a state of panic.

68

Cleo

Today is my day. I've waited my entire life for this.

I will suffer no more fools. Because I know who I am now.

I am Cleopatra Tait.

Not Harris's jilted lover, not Thalia's protector. Cleo. Me. And I'm going to make sure everyone knows that. Today.

The events of the last twenty-four hours have slapped me in the face. Awakened me to my pitiful timidity. As of now, forward movement only.

I am done with that ugly, washed-up old man in the tailored gray suit ruling my life. He's not only destroyed my happiness for my entire adult existence, he's ruined Harris by turning him into a cowering simp.

And I'm done with my traitor of a sister. She may think she knows who she's dealing with, but she couldn't be more naïve. I'm about to show her that when you play with fire, you get burned.

I've wasted enough time bowing to other people's

demands. I will never be intimidated by anyone again. From today onward, my enemies will be afraid of me.

It's time to put an end to this never-ending saga of tragedy. That poor little girl was the first victim, but she's been put to rest, and she can never be brought back. Ryan was next, and he isn't even in the grave yet. I will kill this perpetual cycle of trauma and control.

Time to get this show on the road.

I'm going to end this. For good.

69

Harris

I have very little time to get out of here before my father's hired driver-slash-enforcer arrives. I throw on yesterday's clothes, run some cold water through my hair, and fumble with the hidden camera to remove the memory card. I know where the camera is because my father instructed me to angle it so that the recording could be as incriminating as possible for Thalia. What I don't know is how to retrieve the card. I fumble around, pushing every little button until finally it pops out.

"Got it," I whisper under my breath. No matter what a mess I've made of my life, I won't let my father destroy Thalia's family. This is my fault, and I'm going to fight back. I shudder a bit at the thought. I've never stood up to my father before. It's about time.

So as not to run into any of my father's men on the elevator, I take the hotel stairs, leaping down them two at a time. I've got to get out of here before anyone spots me. I'll never get away from my father's people unless I do it now. This is my only chance.

Reaching the lobby, I hang back and survey the area. A black car is just pulling up to the front entrance. It could be them, or it could be someone else. I can't take any chances. I duck into the Six Seven Restaurant, grab a menu, and slide into a booth. I'll hide amongst the morning diners until I can assess the situation. If I run outside now and it's my father's people, they'll have an easy time grabbing me and shoving me into the car. Then they'll search me for the memory card, which is burning a hole in my inside jacket pocket.

Just as I peek over the top of the menu, my phone buzzes. I ignore it, waiting for the occupants of the black car to come inside. Eventually, a man and woman enter together, laughing, and head to the check-in desk. A hotel porter follows with their luggage. Definitely not my father's people. I take this moment to slip out of the entrance. I press a stack of twenties into the palm of the valet parking attendant, telling him to hurry. He complies, and as soon as I'm alone in my car, I speed away. I don't know where I'm going or what I'm doing, but I'll get to a crowded area, then make some decisions.

As I drive east on Pike Street, I sneak a glance at my phone. It's a text. From Thalia.

She's confirming that she's still coming to my victory party tonight, as we had planned. Fine. Okay. I don't text her back.

If only it would have been Cleo.

Even if she just wanted to yell at me, scream, berate me.

I wouldn't care.

But she'll probably never speak to me again after last night.

My mind wanders as I drive through downtown. Wishes, hopes, regrets… How could I have let Cleo go? She's the only woman I've ever loved. I know that now.

I'm a weak man, a pathetic man, allowing my father to control my life.

She deserves better. But I can change. I can be better.

I have to see her again, if it's the last thing I do. I'll find her. Give it my very best shot, to apologize to her for everything, if she'll let me.

But there's one little thing I need to pick up first.

70

Thalia

I'm desperate to avoid Warren's wrath, but the girls have to get to school. I tiptoe through the door, hoping they're dressed so I can whisk them away without confrontation.

No such luck. They're eating dry cereal in their pajamas at the kitchen counter watching cartoons, hair unbrushed and backpacks unpacked. Of course. I don't know why I thought I could trust Warren to take care of them for even one morning.

"Mommy!" screams Daisy. She jumps up, spilling cereal on the floor, and runs to hug me. Her sister doesn't turn aside from the television.

"Dot's mad at you," says Daisy. "So is Daddy."

"I know, sweetheart. I'm sorry…"

Warren materializes in the kitchen, leaning on the wall with his arms folded.

"Where have you been?" he says. His voice and expression are both flat, without a hint of concern.

"I could ask you the same question," I say.

"Excuse me?"

"Presumably, you've been here all morning, but you haven't tended to the children's needs. Look at them. School starts in twenty minutes and they're not even dressed. I guess I have to do everything around here—"

"ENOUGH!" he thunders. "I work sixty hours a week trying to make a living for this family, and I ask very little of you in return. At the very least, I expect you to take care of the children and be home for dinner. But you've been gallivanting all over town, doing who-knows-what and going who-knows-where, all while complaining that I don't do enough—"

Daisy cries and buries her face in my shirt. I hoist her up and perch her on my hip. She's far too big for this now, but she feels like a shield against Warren's accusations.

"Dot, get dressed. I'll brush your hair. Hurry." I lower Daisy to the floor and grab her hand, pulling her down the hallway.

"No one's going anywhere," commands Warren.

I don't listen. Instead, I groom the girls and bustle them out the front door. Warren braces his hands on the doorjamb and leans out, scrutinizing me, judging me as the girls and I pile into the car. He hates me now, and I deserve it.

As I drive the girls to school, I strategize how I can get full custody of them in the divorce. I can't afford a divorce lawyer, but neither can Warren. I'll need Harris's help. He'll understand, just like he did when he hired the nanny for the girls.

School drop-off is uneventful, and I stop by Starbucks afterwards for a mocha. I sit inside and sip it. I put off going home as long as possible, so that I don't run into Warren again when I go back. He can't stay home all day.

By the time I'm ready to leave, my mocha has gone cold.

I down the last gulp and get back in my car. It's only a few minutes to the house, and when I arrive, I breathe a sigh of relief. Warren's car is gone, so he must have left for work.

I let myself inside, calling his name. He doesn't answer. I check the bedroom just to make sure, but he's definitely gone.

With the house to myself, I make a sandwich and eat in front of the TV. When the morning news ends, I turn it off and clean the breakfast dishes. I still have some time to kill, so I tidy the girls' bedroom. First, I pick up the dirty clothes on the floor, then I make their beds. Daisy's favorite blanket is already on her bed, so I fold it and place it at the foot. Dot's beloved little stuffed mouse is missing, though. She sleeps with it every night, but it's nowhere to be found. It's not under the covers or in the closet. I check the toy box, but it's not there. I crawl on the floor to look under her bed, but it's not there, either.

All of a sudden, I'm overwhelmed with sadness. My nose stings and tears blur my eyes. Where is my baby's little mousey? What will she do without him?

What will she do without me?

Without her father?

Will I leave Warren? Will we get divorced? Will I be sorry?

I sink to the floor and sob. The tears flow like the Duwamish River on a stormy afternoon.

What have I done?

I can't change anything now. The deed is done. I've had the affair. I've slept with a man who isn't my husband, and I will have to live with the consequences.

I pick myself up off the floor, blow my nose, and wipe my eyes until I'm all dried out. Then I get a ladder out of the utility closet, set it up in the hallway, climb it until I almost hit the ceiling, and push open the attic entrance.

There's something up here I need.

Less than five minutes later, I've retrieved the white cotton garment bag and carried it down the ladder. I lay it on my bed, smooth it out, close up the attic, and replace the ladder in the closet.

Back in Warren's and my bedroom, I unzip the garment bag. The red silk gown inside is just as stunning as it was the day Harris had it sent to me. I never wear red, but he insisted. Well, through his assistant, anyway. Iris personally drove the dress over to the house. She told me that Harris had picked it out himself, and that I was to wear it to the victory party after the election. It's a formal event, and he wanted me to look beautiful.

Before she left, she also mentioned that the dress would look best styled with straight hair, worn long and loose. I know nothing about fashion, so I accepted her instructions without question.

I take close to an hour to set up my rarely-used steamer, heat the water, and steam all the wrinkles out of the silk. Then another hour to blow out the curls in my hair and iron it straight. And finally, thirty minutes more to apply makeup — heavier than usual. I hope I look acceptable.

It's not time to go yet, but I want to try on the dress to see how I will look tonight. I slip into the gown, which slides down my body like... well, like silk. This must be how it feels to be wealthy.

Warren always zips the back of my dresses. I don't know how to do it myself. I contort myself, trying to reach behind my head. The zipper goes up three inches, but no more.

The front door slams.

I freeze.

Why is Warren home? I can't let him see me like this. My face flushes and I feel like a fool. A little girl playing dress-up in her mother's clothes.

My eyes light on the closet door, and I make a dash for it. I duck my head and ease behind the hanging clothes, hoping I can't be seen. My hairstyle will be ruined.

"I know you're here, Thalia."

It's not Warren.

It's Cleo.

"Get out of the closet."

"What are you doing here?" I ask, my voice muffled by shirts and jackets.

"I said, get out of the closet."

I poke my head between the hangers to get a look at her. She doesn't seem furious. "How did you get into the house?" I ask.

She laughs. A rude, mean laugh. "Your spare key is under your welcome mat, Thalia. How cunning."

She crosses her arms and glares at me. I stare back, paralyzed. The last thing I want is a confrontation with my sister, dressed in the gown Harris bought for me.

"Get out, or I'll pull you out," she says.

She's serious, so I obey. When I emerge from behind my clothing barricade, she snorts.

"Well, at least we know what he likes," she says. "Get in the car. We're going for a ride."

I try to protest, but she won't take no for an answer.

"Get in the car," she says.

It's an order, not a request, and I find myself responding just like I would have when I was little. Like she's mothering me all over again and I'm a helpless child.

"Let me at least change first," I say.

"Oh no, you're beautiful," she says. "We wouldn't want to change you, would we? Let's go."

She grabs my arm, pulls me out to her car, and pushes

me into the passenger seat. She slides behind the wheel, fires up the car, and screeches out of her parking spot.

"Cleo, where are we going?" I ask. She doesn't answer. "I'm supposed to be at work."

She smirks. I shrink in my seat, feckless and pathetic. Her fingers grip the steering wheel tighter and she takes a hard left.

I don't have a phone, or money, or identification on me. Harris won't know where I am. I'm not even wearing shoes.

I'm scared.

71

Harris

There's nothing more suffocating than a hotel ballroom. My father put together this victory party for me tonight. That is to say, his secretary did. Is this supposed to be fun? Are people supposed to enjoy an event like this? The guests are so stiff, so phony. Everyone angling for a job. I don't know why I never saw it before. All I ever wanted was to follow in my father's footsteps. At least I thought I did. Maybe it's what he wanted for me. I don't even know anymore.

But now… It's like someone pulled a blindfold off my eyes. Looking around this bland, pointless room full of people who don't care about me or know me. Every single person in this room is here because they think I'm a gravy train and they want to get on. They're all just selfish jerks wanting a piece of me.

I hate this place. I hate this career. I hate this life.

But I'm smiling. I can feel it. I feel my hand shaking the mayor's, as if of its own volition. It's like I'm standing outside my body watching. Now I'm slapping someone's back, now I'm laughing just hard enough, but not too hard. All fake.

I'm literally suffocating. It's hot in here.

I can't breathe. I need to get out.

Someone help me. I need Cleo.

Why am I thinking about her? She's gone for me now. I looked everywhere for her: work, home, four different coffee shops, even the library atrium. But I couldn't find her.

No Cleo.

After I win, I'll try again. We'll patch things up. Maybe tomorrow.

I can't wait. I need… someone.

Thalia. Wasn't she supposed to be here tonight? She could help me. Comfort me. I scan the room, overcome by a desperate need to see her. But there's no sign of her. She is supposed to be here! Aren't I paying her to be here?

72

Cleo

This is the longest drive I've ever taken. It seems like we'll never get there.

Thalia's incessant questioning isn't helping. It's making me question myself. This plan I was so confident about this morning seems tenuous now that I've put it into motion.

So much could go wrong, but I have no other option. It's my last-ditch effort at regaining control over my life.

I just need Thalia to stop whimpering so I can keep my head straight.

I can't afford a single mistake today.

73

Harris

Outside on the balcony, I catch a few moments alone. I'm starting to choke. I feel stiff, rigid. I won't be able to speak. If I try, my words will clot together in my throat and strangle me.

The easy, outgoing, relaxed politician is gone, and I'm left alone with myself. The shell of a man I once was, or could have been... I don't even know anymore. But if I have to go back into that ballroom alone, I won't make it.

My knees are locking up. My breath is now shallow and fast.

I need help. I'm calling her.

She answers.

I can barely get her name out.

"C-C-C..." I huff, and try again. "C-C-Cleo..."

"What is it?" she says.

Deep breath. "I need you. Can you come to the hotel?" It's all I can manage. I can't sort my thoughts out enough to explain.

"Well, Mr. Cox, I'm afraid I'm not available right now. I

have a passenger here and I'm taking her out to a very memorable location. I have a special message to deliver. It will be quite enlightening, but I'm afraid I can't reveal any more just now."

I can't comprehend anything she said. I just need her here.

"I need to see you. I can't do this. I can't—" I slump to the cold tile of the balcony floor. "I can feel myself going. Like the collapse. Help me, Cleo. Please, I need to see you…"

"Fine," she says. That's all I need. I feel my nervous system calming down immediately. "If you want to see me, you'll have to come to me."

"But I can't leave," I say weakly.

"Okay, then." She hangs up.

74

Cleo

I knew he'd call. He's made some infuriating mistakes in the last few weeks, but I know Harris better than I know myself.

No doubt he's desperate to make things right with me. We belong together, and this time nothing will keep us apart.

Nothing. And no one.

Without bothering to restrain my impulse, I punch Thalia in the arm. Hard enough to shame, but not hard enough to injure. She winces.

"Sorry," I say. I am, in a way. But she brought this on herself.

My phone rings again. It's Harris.

"I'll go anywhere," he says. "Where are you?" He sounds so small.

"Well, it's pretty far away," I say. "I don't think you should leave your own party to travel out to a dirt road in the middle of nowhere, do you?"

"No," he says, quietly, soberly. He knows exactly what I

mean.

From the passenger seat, Thalia cries out, "Harris?"

"No," he says again, stronger this time. I can hear him shuffling around now, as if he's moving, collecting himself. He'll be leaving that party in about three…

"Do you have Thalia?" he asks.

"If you want to know, you'll have to come and find me. You know where I'll be."

…two…

"Harris!" she screams this time. I slam on the gas.

"Forest Road 46, Harris!" I yell. And disconnect.

…one.

He'll be there.

75

Thalia

My arm hurts. Cleo punched me, hard. If Warren ever did that to me, I'd leave him immediately. For a second, I wish Warren would come and save me until I remember I've effectively left him already.

I'm on my own.

Cleo has gone mad. What does she plan to do with me? First kidnapping me and now driving, driving, driving. She wouldn't actually harm me, would she?

"What are we doing, Cleo?" I ask. "Where are we going? What's Forest Road 46?"

She doesn't answer. She's gripping the steering wheel, leaning so far forward her head almost touches the windshield.

"What's with this car, anyway? Whose is it?" I ask again.

She grumbles under her breath. Weird, like a growl, almost. I have to get her talking, so I can get through to her.

"Cleo," I say. "Cleo." Still nothing.

"CLEO!"

"Shut up, Thalia," she says. Her voice is low. It sounds like a warning.

But it's a start. I won't let up now.

"No, I want to know what is going on. Where are you taking me? What's Forest Road — whatever? And why did Harris call?"

"STOP!" she shouts, pounding the steering wheel. "I told you to shut the hell up! Don't you dare talk to me about Harris. You know nothing about Harris Cox. Nothing!"

Now she's triggered me. I let go, completely reckless. "Harris loves me! He wasn't calling for you, he was looking for me! I'm supposed to be with him. Now. Tonight. It's election night and I'm supposed to be with him!"

Cleo throws her head back and laughs like a maniac. The car swerves into the next lane over, inches away from a deadly collision with an eighteen-wheeler, just like the one Warren used to drive. The driver blares his horn as he sails past. My heart thumps twice its normal speed. Wherever Cleo is taking me, she might kill us both before we get there.

"Do you actually believe that, Thalia?" she says, oblivious to our narrow escape from sudden death. "Or should I say 'Mrs. Warren Edwards'? Or how about 'Mommy'? Do Daisy and Dot know the Senator's son is in love with you? Does the Senator know, for that matter? I mean, really, if you haven't met the family, how serious could it be?"

My face is hot; I'm flushing up to my forehead. Why do I feel so much shame? Does she have a point? No, I know Harris wants to be with me.

I just have to make it out of this car alive.

76

Cleo

I haven't talked to Thalia in the two hours since her ridiculous outburst. The woman is deluded. To think that Harris was doing anything other than following his father's orders, the same as he did with me?

The bulk of this car ride has passed in thick, rigid silence. But I'm not about to break the tension and chat about the weather — drizzle and mist, as usual — just to ease her fears. She does not know what kind of fire she's been playing with. Well, I'm about to change that.

I'll show her exactly how badly she could get burned.

I glance over at her. She's huddled in a ball in the passenger seat, wearing the red dress that would only look good on me. Her head is in her hands and she's shaking. Is she scared? Cold? Or just silently weeping? I don't care. I can't.

We're within striking distance of our destination. The closer I get, the faster my pulse races. My mouth dries out and my sweat runs cold. The scene of the crime comes into view.

I hate this place so much.

It's deserted, just like it was that day. In fact, this is the only way I've ever seen it. It's almost like this stretch of road is my private hell, where no one else ever comes or goes. It will be here, empty, waiting for me until I die.

I stop the car in the middle of the road. I shut off the ignition, but don't bother taking the keys out. There's no one else here.

"Get out," I order my traitorous little sister.

She nudges open the door and stands close to the car, almost hugging it. She won't even move back far enough to shut the door. I get out and look at her across the roof. She just stares off into the distance, forlorn.

I feel the need to protect her.

"Dammit," I whisper. I can't go soft now. "Thalia!"

She turns to me silently, eyelashes wet with mist, or tears, or both. My sister.

"He doesn't love you, you know," I say. "He can't. He only loves me, but he can't have me. So he's trying to turn you into me."

"That's not true," she says, unable to convince herself.

"Look at you! You're like a sad, rumpled version of me after a romp in the boys' locker room at the prom!" She starts to cry. I have another urge to put my arms around her and comfort her. But I have to say what I came here to say.

"You don't want him, anyway, Thal! He's—" I halt. I brought her here for this, but I didn't expect the words to hurt so much coming out.

"What?" she cries. "He's yours? He left you years ago."

"Yes, he's mine! He's always been mine and he always will be. Do you know why he left me, as you say? Do you know?" I pound the roof of the car. "Because he's a murderer, Thalia! A murderer who got away with it!"

"No!" she screams. "You're lying!"

The clouds darken the sky, as if even the sun were hiding from the terrible truth.

"He murdered a child right here, in this spot, where you're standing. And his father covered it up."

"I don't believe you. It's not true."

"I was there."

"Then you're just as guilty. Why didn't you tell anyone? Why didn't you report it yourself? Doesn't that make you just as guilty as Harris?"

"YES!" I shriek. "That's what split us up! The Senator ordered Harris to stay away from me so he'd never get caught! But he never stopped loving me, and I never stopped loving him."

We stand there in drizzly silence for a few minutes, not knowing how to continue. I'm the first to speak.

"How long have you been having an affair with him?"

"Don't call it that. It sounds so... sordid."

I laugh. "Did I raise you to be so naïve? I sheltered you too much. You're a grown woman living in a dream world, thinking a politician with a dirty secret is your knight in shining armor. There's no fairytale at the end of an illicit affair with an unscrupulous public figure, Thalia. I thought I did a better job than that."

"Well, I guess you didn't," she says. "I guess you spent too much time whoring yourself out to every guy who glanced your way. An unpaid hooker like you could never be good enough for Harris. How dare you slander him like that?"

A look of keen understanding spreads across her face, a wise look I've never seen on her before. I don't think I like it.

"It was you," she says. "You planted the threats at his office. You are the one who has been terrorizing him for weeks, scaring him, and stressing him out. I'm going to tell him. He'll never forgive you. He'll hate you forever, just like I do."

A ferocious anger explodes from deep inside and I leap over the car like a wildcat and shove her down to the road. I'm on top of her, screaming, grinding her face in the dirt, desperate to erase the version of me she's trying to become. She's clawing at me, drawing blood. She's sobbing, muddying the ground with her tears. I hate her, I hate myself, I hate Harris.

I roar at the oppressive, gray sky and its tears that never let up, until my roar is matched by a loud, sustained car horn. Both Thalia and I freeze, tattered and broken. We look behind us.

A car has materialized out of the fog, and the man himself is sitting in the driver's seat.

77

Thalia

He's here. I'm saved.

"Harris!" I cry, my voice hoarse. "Harris!"

I push at Cleo, trying to force her off me. I hurt all over.

He'll take me home.

78

Harris

After two hours of tense driving, I'm stiff, tired, and bleary-eyed. Through the mist, I see a twisted pile of raven-haired women on the road ahead of me.

Fear wraps around my heart. Cleo is going to kill her sister.

It's happening, here, all over again. I can feel it. Death on the mountain.

79

Cleo

Harris's car horn blares its warning through the fog, relentless.

I release my grip on Thalia, disentangle myself, and bolt toward him. The car skids to a stop as I trip on a branch and tumble to the dirt.

I scramble back to my feet. At the car, I pull on the driver's side door handle. It's locked. I pound on the window.

"Let me in! Dammit Harris, let me in!

He opens the door and I shove him over to the passenger seat. I clamber in after him and slip behind the wheel. The car is still running.

A shock of stillness chills the air. A frozen moment just before the inevitable occurs. My eyes tunnel in to the forlorn, bedraggled, weeping woman existing on the road a hundred feet ahead.

My blood surges and the world roars back to life. My foot rears up like a cougar before the ambush and slams down on the gas pedal. Like a tragic ancient statue, Thalia stands ready to meet her fate. The metal so close, ready to connect with her, to spread the blood of her body on the silk of her dress.

My eyes are open. I want to see.

Then powerful hands, viselike hands, grip mine and force them, hard, to the right.

We skid.

We miss her by an inch.

We are in the brush.

We thud.

My head hits.

The world is black.

80

Harris

My hand caresses Cleo's elegant, structured face. It's been so long since I touched her. The bump on her forehead is growing by the second. She needs help. She needs medical attention.

I should call someone. My father will know what to do.

My finger hovers above my phone screen, but I can't call him. He is the problem. It's his fault we ended up this way. If Cleo dies…

No, I won't make the same mistake. I call 911 instead and give them our location. They promise to send an ambulance immediately.

But before they get here, I have something to say to Cleo. I feel a mounting sense of urgency. If I don't say it now, I will probably never be alone with her again. No matter how wrong this is, it's my only chance.

"Cleo," I say. She's breathing, but she doesn't seem to hear me. "Cleo," I try again.

81

Cleo

Blink. Blink.
Blurry.
Blink. Blink.
Pain.
Blink.
A tree. So close.
My ears ringing.
Someone is talking.
Who is talking?
The strong hand touches my chin, turns my head.
Harris.
Oh, yes.
Harris is talking.

82

Harris

Her eyes flutter open and she groans. A rush of air escapes me. Relief.

She's alive.

"Cleo, there's something I need to say to you." She gazes through the window, dazed.

"Cleo," I command. "Look at me."

She does. Her eyes snap to attention. She is back.

She tries to talk, but I can't let her. It's my turn now. This is my last chance.

I sound like an idiot, tumbling over my words, but I don't care.

83

Cleo

Pay attention, Cleo.

I shake my head, trying to clear it.

He's grabbing me now, gripping my face in his hands.

I don't want him to touch me. Why won't he stop talking?

Focus, Cleo.

"This is the last chance I'll ever have," he says. He sounds desperate. "Please, listen to me."

And out of his pocket comes a ring. A diamond one.

The one from his safe.

I'm wide awake now.

The ring that was meant for... who? Not Amber. Not Thalia.

"What the hell is that, Harris?" I scream at him.

"They're all going to be here any minute, Cleo, and then I'll never see you again. Please, let me do this now. I meant to do it all those years ago, and I couldn't, and then the accident happened, and then we couldn't see each other anymore, and it's all about to happen again unless I can redo it, fix it all right now. This is my chance."

I laugh at him. Maniacally. He is so deceived if he thinks we can just redo the day of the accident and everything that came after, and make it all okay.

He grabs my hand forcibly and pushes the ring onto it. "Be my wife, Cleo. Be my wife." I'm still laughing. "BE MY WIFE," he yells.

Then suddenly I remember my sister.

I scramble out of the car to go check on her. What could I have been thinking? I almost killed her. I almost let this situation, this place, destroy the only family member I have in this world. But I can't blame it on the place. It's me. It's my fault. My anger, my jealousy. I don't know what drove her to sleep with Harris, but we can sort all that out later. I'm sure I'm to blame somehow for that as well. After all, she's my little sister, and she's my responsibility. She always has been and always will be. In my heart, anyway.

"Thalia!" I yell, as I run up to her. She's lying in a heap on the dirt, weeping, a grown-up version of the little brown-haired girl I held as she lay dying in this spot the last time I was here.

Instinctively, I examine her for injuries, then gather her up in my arms just the way I did when she was little.

Harris's ring on my finger flashes into view.

And all I feel is calm. Strength. Resolve.

I've come so close to destroying what is most dear to me for this complex man. I've spent fifteen of the best years of my life pining for him. I can never take those years back. But neither can I erase the wrong he and I committed together. Nor all the subsequent evil that's resulted.

If I reject Harris's proposal, will that be the end of all this? Can I really just walk away from the Cox family forever, unscathed? The Senator would hardly allow that.

Besides, it would be supremely unfair to drag another innocent soul into this mess. I couldn't expect another man to be with me, with all these dead bodies rotting under the floorboards.

A surge of strength rises in me. I now know exactly what needs to be done, and I'm ready to do it.

I guide my sister into the back seat of the rental car so she can rest for a moment, knowing this time that she will be okay. I take a deep breath and walk back to Harris's car, calmer and more confident than I've ever been. The underlying desperation I've felt vibrating beneath my entire life has burned away. I've made my choice.

I open the car door, straddle Harris in the front seat, and kiss his defeated face with fifteen years of pent-up passion.

"Was that a real proposal?" I ask, probing his soul with my eyes. This is a test.

"Yes," he says. "I've wanted to ask you since the day of the accident, and every day since. I do love you, Cleo. I've destroyed nearly everything I've touched, and I don't care about anything else in my life. It's you, and only you. Forever. If you'll have me."

"Your father will never allow it," I say. Another test.

"To hell with him." He sounds tired, but committed. I'm in.

"Then yes," I say. "I will be your wife. It's about damn time you asked." I kiss him again.

"We do this right," I say, sliding off of his lap onto the seat beside him. "Your father would rather have me dead than part of his family, so we need to bypass him and go straight to the public. He finds out when they do. Until then, we don't leave each other's side."

He nods.

"Presumably, you're going to win the election tonight?"

I say. I can't imagine the Senator would leave this to chance.

"It's a foregone conclusion," he says.

"Even better. You'll be a public figure, which makes it much harder to murder your fiancée in secret. You can announce your engagement at your victory speech."

"I can't make one now," he says. "It's already getting dark, and we're hours away from Seattle. There's no way we'll ever make it back before the party is over."

"True," I say. "Then the three of us drive back together. We'll leave the rental car here. We'll figure out how to pick it up later. I don't want the three of us to be separated until this engagement announcement is made public. For security reasons. Call Iris to let her know what's going on. Then we'll go on television tomorrow morning. I bet she can get you a spot on the local morning show to not only thank the voters, but to make your engagement announcement."

I've gone into whirlwind mode. Perfectly secure. Everything is under control. Finally. After weeks of tussling with the Senator — and years of him controlling my life — I've got the upper hand. And to think, all it took was a simple marriage proposal.

6 Months Later

2019

84

Harris

Cleo insisted upon having the wedding at the Edgewater. To reclaim her power over the place that hosted the worst night of our lives. I never wanted to see the inside of this place again after what I did here. I sank lower than I thought possible. But somehow, amidst my self-destruction, Cleo reached out and rescued me in the most unpredictable way.

I wander through the hotel lobby, running my hand over the river rock that makes up the grand fireplace mantel. How did I ever find the courage to propose to Cleo? And why did she agree to marry me? After everything I've done. And even worse, after seeing how truly evil my father can be. I'm still sick when I remember all that he did, in order to preserve my political career. The career I'm not even sure I want. But it seems to want me, so here I am, a sworn representative in the United States Congress.

Cleo and I are bound through some invisible tether. It must be love. She's always known that, no matter how foolish I've behaved.

We've never spoken of that day on the mountain six months ago. It was nearly a replay of the tragedy in our past, but I thwarted that from happening. Grabbing the steering wheel and forcing the car off the road didn't just save Thalia's life; it changed the entire trajectory of mine. I finally took control.

Maybe that's what gave me the courage to propose.

For fifteen years Cleo waited for me to become my own man, to stop taking orders from my father. Once I saw the error of my ways, I didn't dare squander another minute. I jammed that ring on her finger, and I haven't seen it off since. Cleo has thrown herself into planning this wedding, full of energy, the whirlwind of a woman I always knew she was.

God, I love her.

I'm not good enough for her. But here we are now, getting ready to make our union official. I've practiced saying my vows for months. No matter how nervous I am, I am determined not to stutter today. Nor to collapse again. No. I am going to make it. Cleo's husband, the congressman. I will do this with dignity.

As for my father, he was livid. Anger isn't even the word for how he reacted when I finally saw him the morning after the election. Not only had I been out of contact since the day before, forcing him to cover for me at the victory party, when I dropped by his hotel the next morning, I was with Cleo. For a moment I thought he would kill us both with his bare hands, but he regained his composure so abruptly it was disconcerting. From blind rage to composed politician in the shock of a second. He controlled himself admirably, considering how much hatred he has toward the woman who is minutes away from becoming my wife.

When we told him we were engaged, he congratulated us, but I could tell he was desperate to get me alone. He wanted nothing more than to intimidate and threaten and force me to break it off. But I wouldn't have it. I wouldn't give him the pleasure.

Since then, Cleo has been some sort of magic shield against his wrath. Whenever she is around, he controls himself. Consequently, I make sure she is always around. I am never alone with him anymore. Even when we meet to strategize about political issues, Cleo comes with me. We gave her the title of Senior Political Strategist, so no one can argue. She's even on the payroll.

The lobby lights up a golden pink as the sun sets over Elliott Bay. I watch through the floor-to-ceiling windows as the last sliver of light slips behind the water. The vanishing of it, the absence, breaks open a wave of grief.

For the father I admired.

I wanted so much to look up to him. I respected him. I wanted to be like him, to follow in his footsteps. My eyes are now open to all the evil he has committed over the years. I didn't want to see the truth about how he's gotten where he is and how he stays there, but the truth eventually gets exposed.

The one thing I know is that I will never abuse people the way he has. I will never be like him in that way. In the past, I would have doubted whether I was strong enough to resist the temptation, but I no longer have to worry. I have Cleo to help me with that. She will never allow me to compromise with my father. She provides the strength I never had on my own.

And it's only moments until she's officially mine.

85

Cleo

"Just wear the veil," says Thalia, checking my reflection in the hotel room mirror. "You look... innocent. Fresh. Bridal."

"Just as I've always wanted," I say. "Sorry, sis, but no. Take it off."

The fireplace crackles in the corner, warming the drizzly spring night. Thalia climbs up on the log frame bed, careful not to tread on my silk train. "If you insist," she says. "But I am right about this." She unpins the veil anyway, making sure not to ruin my sleek chignon. She looks me over, air kisses me, and says, "You're gorgeous, anyway."

After the near tragedy on the mountain, Thalia and I wasted no time forgiving and forgetting our transgressions against each other. She had an affair with my man, but I almost ran her over with his car. We were even.

She went back to fix things with Warren, but he'll never know about the affair. That little secret will stay between the three of us: Thalia, Harris, and me.

Thalia lays the veil on the plush red love seat and carefully re-wraps it in tissue paper. "Well, it's almost time," she says. "Are you sure you don't want me to give you away?"

We've had this discussion already. With no father and a dead mother, Thalia is the only family who conceivably could walk me down the aisle. But considering that I raised her, and not the other way around, it makes no sense for her to act as my guardian. No, I had decided to walk down the aisle alone, the way I'd more or less walked through life until now. In less than an hour, I'm going to be Mrs. Harris Cox, and I'll have a whole new dysfunctional family to play with. But I want to go into this with my head held high. Proud. I want everyone to know that this is my choice and I'm making it, in full knowledge of everything that comes along with joining this emerging dynasty.

Before I can answer Thalia, though, a loud rap at the door interrupts us. She takes one look at me in my dress, voluminous skirt arranged around me, and says, "I'll get that."

She opens the door to reveal the one and only Senator William Cox. Come to see me, I take it.

"I'll leave you two alone?" Thalia asks. I nod slightly, and she slips out. No doubt glad to be out of there after everything he's put her through.

"Hello, William," I say, standing tall and pulling my shoulders back. "Did you come to try to talk me out of this one last time?"

"On the contrary, Miss Tait," he says, with an utterly insincere smile. "I came to congratulate you. Welcome you to the family."

"Well, I'm sure you'll be honored to have me." I cock my

head to the side. "I had the pleasure of meeting your brother and sisters. They're so... different from you. Delightful, actually. Like human beings with feelings. Imagine that."

He blinks his eyes hard and clears his throat. Then he readjusts his cufflinks and straightens his tie. Have I touched a nerve? I've never heard the Senator speak about his family; he seems too calculating ever to have been a child.

When Harris introduced his two aunts and one of his uncles to me this morning, I couldn't put them together with the Senator. From what Harris has told me, Jessamyn, Theodore, and Delphine experienced plenty of hardships growing up, but what didn't break them seems only to have made them stronger. And strengthened their bond as a family. Whatever happened to William? Something went wrong with the man.

Looks like I have a new project to work on. The moment Harris and I return from our honeymoon, I will dig into this family and find out what makes them tick.

Knowledge is power. And damned if I'm not going to get it.

Through the door, I hear the faint sound of the string quartet beginning to play. It must be time for the guests to be seated.

"Sounds like that's your cue. You'd better get out and glad-hand those guests. Your campaign donors will be displeased if they don't get the chance to shake your hand today, William."

He turns to go, but hesitates with his hand on the doorknob. "You can call me Senator."

I laugh and say, "You can call me Mrs. Cox."

He leaves, and a slow smile spreads across my face. That malevolent man will never be free to commit his sins in private again. I will watch him, I will expose him, and I will punish him.

As far as Senator William Cox is concerned, I am the stain that won't wash out.

THE END

a psychological thriller
ALTERED
WILL
family
changes
everything...
HOLLY SHEIDENBERGER

Things couldn't possibly be worse.

Or so William Cox believes.

When a cruel tragedy tears his family apart, he has no choice but to beg a shady family friend for help.

He gets what he needs, but at a terrible price.

Against his will, he becomes embroiled in a vile illegal scheme. Trapped by the crimes he's forced to commit, he can't go back to his life without implicating himself.

Will he end the corruption, even if it means endangering the lives of his entire family?

Or… with his newfound status and wealth… does he even really want to?

<u>ALTERED WILL</u>

The new psychological thriller from

Holly Sheidenberger

A prequel to Related By Blood

COMING SOON

Her husband is missing.

Who can she trust?

Lara is desperate to hear from her husband Cameron.
He should be home by now.

He was supposed to meet his recently widowed
brother Jason for lunch. But when he arrived at their
planned location, something felt wrong.

Hours later, Cameron hasn't come home and
he's not answering his phone.

When a late-night knock at the door brings shocking
news, Lara turns to the only person who can help…
her brother-in-law.

But is Jason as selfless as he seems?
Or is he keeping secrets of his own?

<u>THE KINSMAN</u>

A psychological thriller novelette from

Holly Sheidenberger

A standalone thriller

that can be read in about an hour

AVAILABLE NOW

ABOUT THE AUTHOR

Holly Sheidenberger is a former theatre actress. Her experience in creating roles for the stage inspires her to write juicy characters that you love to hate.

She has lived in misty Seattle, sunny Los Angeles, and now makes her home in the Sonoran Desert of Arizona.

Holly is the wife of Hollywood composer and orchestrator Todd Sheidenberger and the mother of their four daughters.